ROSE

MIKE BRYANT

FOAL

Milton, Ontario
http://www.brain-lag.com/

This is a work of fiction. All of the characters, events, and organizations portrayed in this novel are either products of the author's imagination or are used fictitiously.

Brain Lag Publishing
Ontario, Canada
http://www.brain-lag.com/

Copyright © 2021 Mike Bryant. All rights reserved. This material may not be reproduced, displayed, modified or distributed without the express prior written permission of the copyright holder. For permission, contact publishing@brain-lag.com.

Cover artwork by Cynthia Gould

Library and Archives Canada Cataloguing in Publication

Title: Rose / Mike Bryant.
Names: Bryant, Mike, 1970- author.
Identifiers: Canadiana (print) 20200381458 | Canadiana (ebook) 20200381490 | ISBN 9781928011484
   (softcover) | ISBN 9781928011491 (ebook)
Classification: LCC PS8603.R935 R67 2021 | DDC C813/.6—dc23

Content warnings: Death, graphic injuries

Acknowledgements

I would like to thank Sarah Eals and Timothy Carter for suffering through early version of this and helping to remove the terrible.

Thank you also to Katya Carter and Vijay Mehta for being the first to raise your virtual hands and say "ME!" when I asked who wanted a character named after them.

And thanks especially to my long-suffering wife Cynthia Gould, not just for making beautiful cover art but also for endless encouragement when I say ridiculous things like, "I should write a novel!"

One

Most coffins collapse under the weight of the dirt. Hers was no exception.

The wood had split roughly, just to the right of centre, and dirt had poured in, covering most of her body and all of her head. Fortunately, she had no need to breathe.

She worked her right index finger up through the soil and around a wooden shard until she was able to get a grip on it. It took days. It would have been excruciating if she'd been aware she was doing it.

Gradually, she pulled the shard aside. Dirt slipped through the crack, snaked around her wrist, and filled up the space under her forearm.

With a slowness that would have driven a conscious person insane, she bent her arms and moved her fingers, pushing the dirt aside, until she was able to move her hands up in front of her face.

Wiggling her fingers, she bore her hands into the soil, pushing upwards. She worked the pieces of coffin lid up and down and side-to-side until, eventually, she was able to make enough room to squeeze through. Pushing her hands upwards, she displaced enough dirt to allow her to sit and drag her upper body out of the coffin.

With an impossible patience, she pushed forwards and upwards, bending and squeezing her way through the shattered lid. Dirt wound its way downwards to fill up the spaces where she had been. She stretched and her hand broke the surface.

Heavy, cold raindrops landed on her hand but she couldn't feel them.

The slowest part was over. Comparatively rapidly, she wormed her way towards the surface until her arms were free to the elbows. She lay her arms in front of her, against the ground, and pushed, dragging herself upwards until her head emerged.

Dirt caked her hair and rapidly turned it to mud, which streaked her face. Rain filled her empty eye sockets. She re-anchored her hands and pushed down with all of her strength until she was able to get a knee on the edge of the hole. With one last push, she squeezed out of the grave and landed face-first in the mud. The hole she pulled herself out of closed up as the still-freshly-dug soil collapsed in on itself, filling the rest of the coffin.

Another hour of rain would obfuscate her exit hole enough that nobody would ever notice it. She stood and surveyed her surroundings. Despite her lack of eyes, she could see the shadows of trees and headstones silhouetted by blurry, vague lights in the distance.

With a fingernail, she carved at the thread holding her mouth closed. It snapped. She grabbed an end and pulled. It slid through her flesh, snaking up and down through her lips until it was free. She opened her fingers and the wind took the thread away.

She didn't know where she was but she knew where she had to go. Although she had no idea why. She put one shaky foot forward and began to walk.

Two

Katya stood silently in the unfinished nursery, leaning heavily on the empty crib. Heavy rain turned into oblong lenses that melted down the partially-opened window. Some of the rain blew through the screen, turning into mist on its way into the house. The wind and cold moisture on her skin should have been uncomfortable. Or maybe pleasant. She couldn't remember. The scent of wet earth outside filled the room. She used to love that smell. She used to love the smell of fresh paint, too. A smell which once dominated the room. But no longer, despite the partially-painted wall and the crusty, bone-dry roller still propped up in the corner.

As she stared into the crib, still sitting askew in the middle of the room, waiting for the return of a painter who wasn't coming, she reached up to her chest. Through the folds of her housecoat, she ran a finger down her scar. The wound was no longer sore but the bone beneath it still ached.

"Katya?" the voice of her husband, Vijay, echoed

from down the hall. His soft footsteps grew louder. The floorboards creaked. "Kat?"

She heard him nearly pass by the nursery but then stop. "Sweetie?"

"Hey," she said, barely above a whisper.

Vijay stepped into the room, pressed himself gently against her back and put his arm around her, his hand on her stomach. She placed her hand over his.

"You okay?" he asked. He knew it was a stupid question. She shook her head.

"I really wish you'd let me finish decorating this room," he said.

"No," she said. "Not until I'm ready again."

"Then let me undecorate it," he said.

"What, and just give up?"

"No, not forever. Just for now. I'll tear it all down and start again when the time is right."

Katya leaned to the side and turned her head in order to frown at him. "That seems like a waste of time and money."

"Who cares?"

"Who cares?" Katya repeated, incredulously. "When did you stop caring about wasting money?"

"Just now," Vijay said, stepping around to the other side of the crib. He was wearing a casual but not-too-casual outfit and was freshly shaved. The middle-of-the-road look that was most likely to avoid getting him randomly selected for a search at the airport. "Come on. Let's trash it all. Hell, let's burn this whole place to the ground. Whaddya say? Better Living Through Arson. Just send three payments of twenty-one ninety-nine for my exclusive information guide."

Katya grinned, despite herself.

"Is that a smile I see?" said Vijay. "Does this mean you're on board with torching the place?"

"I can see the appeal," she said. "But my heart's just not in it."

"Maybe it needs to catch up with the rest of you," said Vijay. "I mean, it is a lot newer."

Katya exhaled sharply through her nose in an almost-laugh that failed to land. Vijay considered it to be progress.

"Isn't your flight in like three hours?" she asked. "You should be out the door by now."

"Yeah. Amar just texted. He'll be here any minute."

She nodded.

"I don't have to go," he said. "I'm sure I can convince them to push it back."

"No," she said. "It's your job. It's important. And I'll be fine."

"Are you sure?"

"It's just until the day after tomorrow. I can handle it."

"I just wish I could be there for you when you go back to work tomorrow."

"Really, I'll be fine."

"That almost sounded convincing."

"I'm almost convinced."

Vijay nodded, walked around the crib, kissed her on the cheek, and left the room to go downstairs.

Katya sighed and followed him. She settled herself down on the sofa and turned on the TV only to be met with a lot of nothing.

"TV's out again," she called out. "When are they going to replace that cable?"

"I'll call them again tomorrow," Vijay said on his way through the living room. He slipped his shoes on and walked toward the back door. "I'll reattach it again now. Hopefully it holds until they can get out here."

"Thanks," she said and he went out back.

She dragged herself off the couch, walked across the living room and looked out the front window. The neighbourhood was almost entirely obscured by the rain and the darkness. Streetlights were not considered a priority except on main streets.

Katya and Vijay lived in a quiet neighbourhood in an old single-family home in the extreme northwest corner of Port Langston, the largest town in Langston county. It was an old town of about 30,000 inhabitants, and it had never actually been a port. The town was named after its founder, Eli Langston, who had high hopes of turning it into a center of trade and commerce. But as it turned out, people had little to no ambition to make the trek all the way up the Langston River and around Langston Falls just for the tiny amount of business that trek might bring them when larger, more profitable ports were much closer by. Eli Langston attributed this to a failing of moral character in his fellow men. Port Langston featured a large park, shockingly not called Langston Park, but Rebecca Langston Park, after a suffragette descendant of Eli Langston. Rebecca Langston Park featured a disused bandshell on one side of it and an old, disarmed, Civil War cannon on the other. The cannon was displayed along with a plaque denoting the Battle of Langston Fields which it claimed had taken place right here on this very piece of land. Neither historians nor archaeologists had ever found any evidence that the Battle of Langston Fields had ever taken place. Yet the cannon and its probably apocryphal plaque persisted.

Port Hackett was the second largest town on Port Langston. Named after Charlie Hackett, a well-known gambler and moonshiner, Port Hackett was an actual port when it sprang up during Prohibition. At the time, it was used to smuggle Charlie Hackett's wares out of

Port Langston to the larger cities downriver, past Langston Falls. Eli Langston would not have approved of Charlie Hackett's activities, despite his get-up-and-go attitude. The circumstances surrounding the town's founding were facts which many of its citizens were embarrassed by and loath to admit. Port Hackett was on the opposite side of Lake Langston, but situated further south so the owners of lakefront property in either town didn't have to have their very expensive views ruined by each other. Port Hackett had a considerably larger park than Port Langston, but no bandshell. Nor did they have a cannon in the park. A fact that was cause for great concern by many of the denizens of Port Hackett. The Venn diagram displaying the denizens of Port Hackett who were irked by the town's degenerate history compared to the ones who were jealous of Port Langston's cannon was a circle. Both towns were surrounded by, and permeated with, lush, old-growth forest.

Lightning flashed, revealing a figure standing beside the tree on the boulevard. Katya frowned and stepped closer to the window. When the sky lit up again, the figure had moved closer. It stood in the middle of the yard, hands hanging at its sides, mouth agape, face pale and eyes dark.

The TV signal became clear. The room echoed with the sounds of the moaning hordes of undead shambling across the screen.

Katya continued to peer into the darkness, the rain pouring down. From just outside the window, a beam of light shot upward, illuminating the figure. The side of its head was cracked open and brains spilled down over its shoulders. It choked and blood streamed from its mouth, down onto its chest.

Katya took three steps to the left, opened the door

and said, "Amar, don't you have enough sense to come in out of the rain?"

"Hey, Kat," said Amar, turning off the flashlight and coming inside.

"You look different," she said, muting the TV. "Have you done something with your hair?"

"No, I had my ankle bracelet removed," he said, lifting his leg and pulling up his pant leg. "It feels like freedom. I can actually leave my house."

She heard the back door open and Vijay's footsteps come in.

"And yet you never left the house before you got arrested," she said.

"Well, I had an X-Box."

"And you don't now?"

"No, they took it. It counts as a computer."

"So what did we learn about hacking into military computers?"

"Use better proxies," said Amar.

Vijay stepped into the hallway as Katya shook her head and rolled her eyes, hoping that Amar was joking. He was lucky he was underage when he tried to impress his little hacker friends, or he'd have gotten a lot more than house arrest and probation.

"Hey, there you—what the actual hell, bro?" Vijay said.

"What?"

"Why are there brains spilling out of your head?"

"I was working on a new makeup and I wanted to see how well it stood up to the rain."

"You couldn't just use the shower?" said Vijay.

"Real movie sets don't use showers," said Amar.

"Real movie sets don't use real rain, either."

"It's technical. You wouldn't understand."

"I would like to present an alternate order of

events," said Vijay, collecting his suitcase. "One in which you forgot you were supposed to give me a ride to the airport and you left the house in a hurry with no time to remove your makeup."

Amar stared at him for a moment. "That depends on whether we're in the original or the J. J. Abrams timeline."

"Uh-huh," said Vijay. "So you're going to wear that to the airport?"

"Sure. I'm not the one flying. I'm not even getting out of the car."

"That's a good plan," said Vijay. "Stick with it."

"I have to say, I'm actually impressed that you turned your house arrest into an opportunity to learn something potentially useful," said Katya, gesturing to the brains.

"Thank you, Kat," Amar said. "This is why you're my favourite sister-in-law."

"Only sister-in-law," said Vijay.

"With one this good, why would I need another?"

"Aww. I'd hug you, but," Katya gestured to her chest.

"No worries," said Amar.

"Also, your guts are hanging out and it's gross."

"I'll meet you at the car," said Vijay, standing up.

"Okay. You take care of yourself, Kat," Amar said.

"And you stay out of trouble," she said, as he stepped back out into the rain.

"I promise nothing," Amar shouted back on his way to the car.

Vijay took Katya's hand and once again asked her if she was sure she'd be okay.

"I'm fine," said Katya, in a not-entirely-convincing tone. Vijay gave her his best stern look, one eyebrow raised. "I'm fine," she repeated, with more feeling. "Really. It's two days. I'll live."

"Okay," said Vijay. "If you're sure."

"I'm sure."

"All right," Vijay said. He kissed her and was off to the car.

Katya lowered herself into the well-worn groove on her side of the sofa and watched zombies silently terrorizing the nice people of Anytown. She hovered her thumb over the mute button, but thought better of it. She closed her eyes, relaxed, and enjoyed the sounds of the rain. She may have drifted off to sleep, but she couldn't be sure. She had been doing that a lot lately, mostly due to the medication. But whether she was sleeping or just blissed out, enjoying the rain, her relaxing moment was ended by a loud and slow knock at the door.

Katya started, looked around, and took a moment to get her bearings. The knock sounded again.

"What fresh hell is this?" she said, dragging herself off of the sofa. Pulling her robe tight around her, she shuffled to the door and stood on tiptoe to look through the little window. She saw a shock of frizzy red hair, much like her own but with considerably more grey mixed in with it.

"Mom?" she said as she opened the door.

Aileen Carter, mother of Katya, kept her crisp, black suit dry with a crisp, black umbrella. Her Fluevogs matched her bright, green eyes. They peered at Katya from above a tight, severe expression.

"He actually went?" she said, her Scottish brogue still not entirely dulled from her years of living in the colonies.

"Yeah, of course."

"I can't believe he'd leave you after all you've been through," she said, stepping inside and shaking her umbrella, sending rainwater flying.

"Mom, it's two days. I'll be fine."

"That's what your father did, you know. He went away on a business trip and never came back. He met some floozy cocktail waitress and he never came home."

Katya's father, Adrik Gagarin, and Aileen had been happily unmarried for thirty-three years. Aileen was the cocktail waitress he'd run off with. Not away from anybody else, though. He was currently at home watching crime dramas, not daring to impede on mother/daughter night.

"Come on in, Mom," said Katya to her mother, who had already kicked off her shoes and made a beeline to the liquor cabinet, where she was pouring herself a single malt.

"That hits the spot," she said. "Say what you want about that Vijay character, he knows his booze."

"He does."

"Questionable taste in women, though," she said, settling into Vijay's favourite recliner.

"Leapin' lizards, Miss Hannigan," Katya said, settling herself back into her sofa groove.

"Hey, there's that sense of humour I remember," said Aileen.

"Don't get used to it."

"It'll come back," said Aileen. "In time."

Katya nodded, not sure she believed it.

"When was the last time you left the house?"

"Uh... last Friday was garbage day," said Katya. "So Thursday night."

"I'm not sure that counts."

"It counts a little. Also, the cable keeps going out so I have to go out back to reattach it."

"You definitely need to get out more," said Aileen. "Maybe get you on Tinder or something."

"Vijay would love that."

"I'm sure he'd appreciate having your sullen face out of the house occasionally," said Aileen. "It's quite simple. You just poke at pictures of gentlemen and you get a selection of free, bespoke, penile art and maybe a free meal or two. I'm told it's all the rage. I can see why."

"Or I could just go back to work tomorrow."

"I suppose you could do that," Aileen said, nodding. "If you want to be a corporate sellout, man."

"Mom, you're an accountant."

"A badass accountant."

"Of that, I have no doubt."

There was a pause. Aileen filled it by investigating the legs on her Bruichladdich.

"Are you going to be okay?" she asked. "Going back to work?"

"No."

"Well, that is unfortunate," said Aileen. "I guess you've got about ten hours to nut up, then."

"I'm sure the doctor would give me more time off if I asked."

"What about the hit to your finances?"

"We're fine."

"Define 'fine'," Aileen said.

"The bank isn't currently trying to break down the door with a battering ram," Katya said.

"Well, that sounds like all of your ducks are in a row, then."

"Absolutely," said Katya. "We're in debt up to our eyeballs and behind on the mortgage but at least we've got a cool, dried-up paint roller."

"Then I suppose employment is totally optional."

"Obviously," said Katya, followed by a sigh. "Vijay put you up to this, didn't he?"

"Of course not. You know we don't get along."
"You'd trade me in for him if you could."
"In a second," said Aileen.
"I knew it."
"Good thing I get you both."
"Yep," said Katya. "You're stuck with me."
"I wouldn't have it any other way," Aileen said. She took the final swig of her drink. "He's putting up a brave front, but he's worried."
"I know."
"So that's settled, then."

Three

The urge to keep going was powerful. But something told her she should avoid being noticed. That's why she stepped back behind the tree.

The headlights were far away but she was slow moving. She waited for the car to pass before climbing out of the ditch and stepping onto the side of the road.

Out here there were no streetlights. Only the moon lit her way. But she didn't need to see.

She walked across the road, the pavement rough on her bare feet, and slid into the ditch on the other side. The ground sloped downward and she followed it, weaving around trees and pushing her way through bushes and brambles, her dress getting caught and snagged along the way. Her feet sucked into the mud, occasionally pulling her down to her hands and knees. The mud got everywhere.

She continued on until she came to a creek. There, she paused and looked around for a crossing. There wasn't one. On unsteady legs, she waded across.

As she climbed up the bank on the other side, the sky

began to brighten. She continued to walk until she came upon another road. The sun had risen too high for her to cross unnoticed if anyone happened by, so she turned back, crawled under a bush, and waited. All the while, the urge to walk towards her unknown destination pulled at her. But she sat and awaited the darkness.

Four

Katya pulled into the parking lot of her branch of LRG National Bank and parked. Her breastbone was throbbing with a dull ache. She sighed and checked her purse for her security pass for the fifth time that day. She closed her eyes, practiced her deep breathing, and got out of the car. At the employee entrance, she paused, pass in hand, and stared at the security sensor. Closing her eyes, she took another deep, slow breath. She exhaled, beeped her card, and opened the door. She got barely one step inside when her vision was suddenly filled by a large, grey face with an exaggerated downturned mouth. The face made a childlike, drawn-out sad noise, but the eyes didn't match the sound or the mouth. The face was accompanied by the smell of perfume failing to cover up stale, unfiltered cigarettes.

"Katie," said the face, extending the last syllable.

"Katya," said Katya, not for the first time. "Hi, Tammy."

"It's so good to see you back," said Tammy.

"Thanks," Katya said, knowing that it wasn't. Nonetheless, she smiled and stepped around her. "It's good to be back. Nice to see you." She hated to lie three times in rapid succession, but workplace etiquette demanded it.

She continued down the short hallway, past the break room, and into the bank, proper.

Tammy, on her heels, announced, "Look, everyone. Katie's back!"

"Katya," said Katya.

The other employees waved and said variants of, "Welcome back." Katya knew all of them but one. The new one was an older, balding man in an ill-fitting brown suit.

"Katya. I've heard so much about you from Tammy here," he said, approaching her with his hand outstretched. As he approached, the light glimmered off of his cufflinks. They were the only pieces of flair in his otherwise dull and businesslike ensemble.

"Oh, have you?" said Katya, smiling. "That's great."

"I'm Gord Macalier," he said, shaking her hand. As they shook, she noticed that the cufflinks were gold crosses. Katya guessed that he and Tammy had quickly become bestest work buddies. "I replaced Doug as the new Branch Manager a couple of weeks ago."

"Oh, well, it's a pleasure to meet you. Say, those are great cufflinks," she said.

"Oh, these?" he said, holding one of them up for inspection. "These were a little gift from my church's youth group. Just a little show of appreciation for my years of volunteer service."

"Oh, that's wonderful," said Katya. "You must be very proud."

"I don't really believe in pride, as such, but the kids wanted to show me their respect, so I couldn't really say no, could I?"

"Well, if it's for the kids..."

"Exactly," said Gord, beaming with pride.

"Speaking of kids, isn't it brave of her to come back so soon? After her..." Tammy glanced down at Katya's belly. "...procedure?"

"Uh... thanks," Katya said.

"I mean, it's not a choice that I would have made," said Tammy. "But I think you're so brave to live with your decision, no matter what."

"You wouldn't have had an emergency heart transplant?" Katya said.

"Well, I mean that was a miracle, obviously..." said Tammy.

"Obviously," said Katya.

"But I meant the... You know. Other... situation."

Gord frowned and shook his head, almost imperceptibly. But Katya saw it. Tammy's plan was working. What had she told him previously?

"Losing my baby, you mean."

"Yes, well... I didn't want to—"

"It wasn't exactly a choice, Tammy," Katya said.

"Well, I guess that's between you and..." Tammy glanced upwards briefly, then shrugged. "Someone."

Tammy knew better than to bring up religion in the office, and yet somehow always managed to bring it up without actually bringing it up.

"The gunman?"

Tammy's mouth hung open and she made hesitant, vaguely grunting noises, unsure how to process that or turn it to her advantage.

"We're just all glad that you're okay," said Gord. "Isn't that right, Tammy?"

"Oh, yes," Tammy said, smiling again. "Of course. That's what really matters."

"Well, thank you both," said Katya. "But if you'll excuse me, I should look over my itinerary for the day before we open."

"Yes, you'll want to get back to pulling your weight, I'm sure," said Tammy.

"Of course," said Gord. "Seeing as it's your first day back, I've made sure to have them go easy on you. We'll get you ramped back up to your usual schedule over the next couple of weeks."

"Thank you. I appreciate that," said Katya.

Her office was cold and beige. The floor-to-ceiling interior windows were frosted except for two 6-inch-wide strips. One at about standing eye level, and one just above sitting eye level. Which meant she only felt a little bit like a zoo animal, but the feeling was more pronounced after several weeks of darkened rooms and heavy blankets. The carpet had been recently redone in a quiet, inoffensive beige, and it filled the entire bank with that fresh, chemical-but-not-entirely-unpleasant scent. She looked at her schedule for the day and saw that Gord wasn't kidding when he said it was light. Only six clients over the course of the day. Now she'd have to find some busywork in between.

It was just after lunch time and she was dealing with her fourth client of the day. She was explaining to Mr. Lea the details of his consolidation loan when Tammy peered through the uppermost unfrosted strip. Katya ignored her and went about her business while Tammy tapped gently on the glass. Undeterred, Tammy opened the door and stuck her head in.

"Knock-knock," she sing-songed. Then to Mr. Lea she said, "I'm so sorry, I just have to borrow our Katie for a moment."

"Katya," said Katya.

"That's fine," Mr. Lea said.

"You have a visitor," said Tammy, barely containing her excitement, squeaking like a chew toy on the last word.

Katya craned her neck up to look through the clear portion of the glass, wondering if Vijay had returned home early to surprise her. Instead, she saw a very thin woman facing away from her. The woman wore an angular, dark blue suit jacket with a white blouse and a calf-length skirt. Her hair was pulled back into a severe bun. She turned and looked at Katya. Her downturned lips were thin and pale. She was the sort of person who had appeared to be in her forties since she was a teenager. Tammy looked at her in admiration, then back at Katya in excitement.

"It's Pamela Harrington," Tammy whispered as if she was about to burst.

Katya avoided swearing out loud in front of a client. "So it is."

"I didn't know you knew her."

"She's a neighbour."

Mr. Lea regarded Pamela Harrington with curiosity.

"Tell her I'll talk to her as soon as I'm done here," said Katya.

"You really shouldn't keep her waiting."

"I'm sure she'll be fine," said Katya. "Now if you'll excuse me, I have a client."

"Oh, of course," said Tammy, and she scuttled off.

"Okay, where were we?" Katya asked. "Oh, yes. So your interest rate will be—"

"Sorry, I've got to ask," said Mr. Lea. "Is she some sort of celebrity?"

"She certainly thinks so," said Katya. "She runs my neighbourhood's HOA. Mostly because nobody else wants to. And apparently she's a big wheel down at the Fellowship."

"Does her SUV have a stick figure family?"

"You know, I think it actually does," Katya said. "And a 'My Kid is an Honour Student' bumper sticker."

"I was a dishonour student, myself," said Mr. Lea. "Of course, that might explain my credit rating."

A few minutes later, papers signed and hands shaken, Mr. Lea was out the door and Katya found herself standing in front of Pamela Harrington.

"I'm sorry to bother you at work, but you're a difficult woman to get a hold of," said Pamela.

That's by design, Katya thought, but she didn't say it. "Well, I've been having some health problems," she said.

"I am aware of that," said Pamela. "But I wouldn't have to bother you if your boyfriend were more reasonable."

"Is that so?"

"I'll get right to the point," Pamela said. "You need to paint your door."

"I just painted it a few months ago."

"You need to repaint it."

"I'm sure it's fine."

"It is not fine. It's red."

"And?"

"And red is not one of the approved colors," said Pamela. "Approved colors are white, beige, or certain pre-selected natural wood grains."

"Yes, I know," said Katya. "And the paints must be supplied by United Paint Supply."

"So you are aware of the rules," said Pamela.

"Isn't that the store your sister owns?"

"What are you implying? Nothing actionable, I hope."

"Just an observation," Katya said.

"Listen, Miss Carter," Pamela said, "I don't want to

bother you in your current state, but I've tried speaking with your boyfriend—"

"Husband," said Katya.

"—and he simply won't listen to reason. But that's to be expected, I suppose."

"Why is that to be expected?"

"I was willing to give him the benefit of the doubt at first. I could live with the language barrier but it seems he's just using that as an excuse."

"What language barrier?" said Katya.

"Well, I don't mean to be rude, but his accent is quite thick."

"He doesn't have an accent."

"Perhaps you've grown used to it," said Pamela.

"He was born here," said Katya. "He has no accent."

Pamela gave her a cold, insincere smile. "I know that you'll listen to reason. You have a career so you understand why we have rules. Rules are rules and they are in place for a reason and you are in violation of one of the rules of the Home Owner's Association. I know you don't want to violate the rules, do you, Miss Carter?"

"Certainly not," said Katya.

"And you know that there are consequences if they're not followed. Don't you, Miss Carter?"

"Sure."

"That's good to hear," said Pamela. "So you'll have the door returned to an approved colour by Friday?"

"No."

"I'm sorry?"

"Well, it's just..."

"What?"

"We're not members of the HOA."

Pamela's eyes widened. Her face turned red and a vein on her temple throbbed.

"Everyone in the neighbourhood is a member of the HOA."

"Not us," said Katya. "We lived there before it went into effect and we never joined."

"I am familiar with the history of the neighbourhood," said Pamela. "I've lived there a long time. I started the Home Owner's Association. Do not lecture me about the history of the neighbourhood."

"I wasn't. I was just pointing out that—"

"You and that boyfriend of yours are the final holdout. Everybody else has joined. Why not you? Do you think you're special? Is that it?"

"No, we just don't want to join."

"So you think the rules do not apply to you?"

"They literally don't."

"Miss Carter, the Homeowner's Association exists for the benefit of the entire community," said Pamela. "You don't want to bring down the entire community, do you?"

"Of course not, it's just—"

"What, Miss Carter? It's just what?"

"I want a red door."

Pamela Harrington glared at Katya, nostrils flaring. "This is not over," she said before storming out.

Katya's hand went to her chest. With her other hand, she leaned on one of the waiting area chairs. She was suddenly exhausted.

"Oh, my heavens, isn't she amazing?" Tammy said, descending on Katya.

"What?"

"Pamela Harrington," said Tammy. "Isn't she incredible?"

"That's one word for it."

Five

It rained again that night. Katya cocooned herself in blankets on the sofa with the window open just enough to smell the rain. The TV was on but she wasn't really watching it when her mother called to check up on her.

"How was the first day back?"

"Ugh," Katya said.

"That good, was it?"

"It was fine," said Katya. "But Tammy is still Tammy."

"Which one is Tammy?"

"The one who tries to drag everybody else down at every turn but disguises it as concern and support."

"The backhanded complimenter?"

"More like the backstabbing implier. She knows exactly what to say so that other people understand what she's getting at but you'd have no leg to stand on in an HR sense. It all sounds like she's just being nice and if you have a problem with it then the problem must be you."

"A Sith Lord with a clip board."

"Oh, she's nowhere near clever enough to be a Sith Lord."

"A Slytherin not deliverin'?"

"Something like that," said Katya, grinning. "Wait."

"What is it?"

Katya sat up and said, "I just heard a noise."

"What sort of noise?" Aileen asked.

"I think someone's on my porch," Katya said, moving the phone away from her ear so she could listen for more noises from outside.

"Did you order Indian while Vijay was away?"

"No," said Katya. "Well, yes, but I ate it already." She listened for a moment but heard only the rain. "Hmm. Maybe it was just a raccoon or something."

"Perhaps a late flyer delivery?"

"I didn't hear the mailbox," said Katya. "Hang on... I think someone's in the alley."

Katya crawled out from her blanket oasis and walked to the side window. She pushed it farther open and put her face against the screen. It was too dark out to see anything but as she looked towards the front of the house, a brief flash of lightning revealed movement. Or did it? She wasn't sure.

"Hang on a second, Mom," she said to the phone. She went to the front door and tried to turn on the porch light but it didn't come on. She rose up on tiptoe and peered out the little window at the top of the door. Once again, she thought she caught a glimpse of movement on the porch, this time to her right, by the large front window on the side where the alley was. She went to that side of the window and pulled the drapes to the side just enough to peek out. She saw nothing. Or maybe a shadow? It was too difficult to tell. Until another flash of lightning lit up a ghastly pair of eyes peering back at her from a ghostly, pale, skull-like face. She stifled a scream, pulled back the drapes, and crouched.

The sound of sharp, deliberate footsteps thudded across the porch and stopped in front of the door. Three loud, cracking knocks sounded out. Katya froze.

Her mother's voice sounded from the phone, thin and tinny, barely audible over the rain. "Honey? Are you there?"

Katya stared at the door, eyes wide with terror as her mother continued to call her. "Katya? Katya! What's going on?"

She looked at the phone in her hand and began to raise it slowly to her face. The three knocks sounded again. She inhaled sharply and stared at the door. She brought the phone to her ear and whispered, "Mom? I've got to go."

"Is someone there?"

"Yeah."

"Who is it? Are you okay?"

"You know that Sith Lord?"

"Yes?"

"It's the Emperor."

Three hard knocks sounded once more. Katya disconnected, stood up, and went to the door.

"Hello, Pamela," she said as she opened it.

"It's Mrs. Harrington," said Pamela. "I use your honorific, Miss Carter. I expect the same respect in return."

"Fine. Mrs. Harrington," said Katya. "How can I help you?"

"I have excellent news for you," said Pamela. "The Home Owner's Association has reviewed your case and come up with an alternative solution."

"What are you talking about?"

"The association has agreed to pay your dues, backdated to its inception, making you a retroactive member with all of the perks and privileges contained therein. This comes with automatic seniority in the association dating back to the day you first joined."

"Pamela, I told you we don't want to join."

"Nonsense. This is better for everybody," said Pamela. "I had to pull in quite a number of favours to do this for you, as a lot of people don't think your seniority should be backdated. But I managed to convince them that it was for the best."

"You really didn't need to—"

"Now, of course, with these advantages come certain responsibilities, i.e., the color of your front door which, I note, is still in violation of the code. But the good news is that if you correct this oversight by five p.m. Friday, you won't be obligated to pay the outstanding retroactively-paid dues."

"I'm sorry, what?"

Pamela pulled a pile of papers out of her satchel and handed them to Katya. "I've had the agreement written up and notarized. This is your copy. You'll also find copies of the receipts of payment for your membership dues as well as the loan agreement that we drafted in order to allow you to have your dues paid for the past five years."

"This is ridiculous," Katya said, her hand moving to her chest.

"I disagree," said Pamela. "As does the Association's board. We've given you a very generous interest rate. Although after five years, it's built up to quite a sum. We are willing to waive the principal if you bring your house up to code. We are not, however, able to waive the interest. I'm sure you'll understand. The board isn't made of money, after all. I'm sure you can get a loan, considering your job. You seem the type to take advantage of your connections."

"This isn't legal," said Katya, quietly.

"I can assure you it is. My husband is a lawyer and he's put quite a number of billable hours into this. We have, of course, added those to the principal, as I'm sure you'll see. Assuming you bother to actually read the agreement," said Pamela. "Which I can't force you to do."

"But..."

"The Association appreciates your cooperation in this matter. Good day, Miss Carter," she said, and she turned to leave. She stopped with one foot on the stairs and turned back. "And tell your friend to get in out of the rain. She'll catch her death of cold."

"My friend?"

"Not that it matters to me, but it's not Halloween. Which is, of course, the only day in which the wearing of a costume is acceptable," said Pamela. "And then, only costumes from the approved list are allowed, which I can assure you, hers is not. She'll frighten the children, looking like that."

"What friend?"

"Whoever that was standing on your porch when I pulled up. She looked like she needed a bath. Honestly, the company you people keep. But that's none of my business."

She walked quickly to her car and drove away, leaving Katya confused and angry.

Katya stood in the doorway, holding the pile of papers in one hand and her phone in the other. She stared at the spot where Pamela's car had been, the rain blotting out all other sounds. Lightning illuminated the area and for a moment Katya thought she saw a figure standing across the road, looking at her from behind a tree. It appeared to be a pale girl with long dark hair, black, recessed eyes, and a dirty, formerly white dress. Katya focused on the spot, trying to see through the rain and the darkness when another lightning bolt flashed across the sky. There was nobody there. Katya felt a deep sense of unease. She was startled by a sudden vibration and buzzing noise from her hand. She jumped and dropped her phone.

Her phone buzzed and lit up again, revealing a picture of she and her mother laughing after, as Aileen would say, "a lot of a couple of Chardonnays." She picked up the phone and answered it. "Mom?"

"Okay, what's going on?"

"Ugh, it's nothing," Katya said, stepping inside and closing the door. "Just your friendly neighbourhood führer trying to invade." She didn't feel as nonchalant as she sounded.

"I'm sorry?"

"That woman I told you about. The one who runs the HOA."

"What's she upset about this time?" Aileen asked. "Did she want to remove your tongue for speaking out against the stonings?"

"No, she's upset about our red door."

"I should think so," said Aileen. "Only harlots and Democrats have red doors."

"Is that so?"

"Yes, I read it in Horrid Fusspot Quarterly."

"I must have missed that issue," said Katya.

"I'm sure the back issues are online. Not that nice girls use computers."

Katya made a sound not entirely unlike a chuckle.

"Are you okay, sweetheart?"

"Yeah, I'm fine," Katya said, walking back to the sofa.

"Indeed, you sound perfectly untroubled."

"I'm just really tired," she said, kneeling on the sofa and pushing the blankets away from her spot. "Today took a round out of me."

"Okay, I'll let you go," Aileen said. "I'm a phone call away."

"I know. Thanks."

She crawled back into her sofa nest and pulled the blankets around her. She put her hand to her chest scar, closed her eyes, and took a deep breath. She turned on the TV. And the signal was, once again, out.

Katya moaned lightly and considered her options. It was too early to go to bed and she didn't think she could concentrate on a book. If the TV was out, then so was the Internet. Besides, the Internet Outrage Machine was only liable to angry up the blood. She sighed, crawled out of her nest, put her shoes on, and went to the back door. A flashlight and umbrella lived on a shelf beside the door, left there by Vijay for just such an occasion. She took them and went out into the cold, wet night. The rain pattered on the umbrella and mud squished under her shoes as she crossed the back yard to the utility pole where the cable came in. Once again, the rusted-out connector had come undone. The too-small piece of duct tape that had studiously held it together for several years was a vaguely sticky lump of grey goo criss-crossed with soaking-wet threads. She raised her shoulder to hold the umbrella against her neck, squeezed the flashlight under her arm, and pulled the stray cable to the connector. They held together hesitantly for a moment before popping apart.

Katya bent down and searched the unkempt garden for a rock. She found one heavy and flat enough that it should be able to do the job. She pulled the cable behind one of the slats in the privacy fence, stretched the connector-end to the same spot, pushed them together, and set them down on a horizontal mid-fence beam. She set the rock on top. It held.

"Look at me, being an expert electrician," she said.

She turned around to head back inside but found her way blocked by a person. Under the sound of the rain, the person had gotten nearly within touching distance of Katya without being heard. It was the girl she thought she had seen watching her earlier. Her white dress was caked in mud, ground in so hard that the rain wasn't helping. Her hair was the same, knotted and tangled, with clumps of dirt ground in, oozing slowly down her face and neck. Her skin was deathly white. Her bare feet had sucked into the muck of the garden, her toes turned inwards, one leg turned far to one side. Her lips were black, as were her empty eye-sockets which, despite their lack of eyes, looked directly at Katya. The top two buttons on her dress were undone and she had a long tear down the front, revealing a scar that matched Katya's.

She took a shaky, lurching step forwards as she spoke. Her voice was low and gravelly as she pointed a thin, bony finger at Katya.

"You have my heart," she said.

Katya screamed, dropped the flashlight, and swung hard at the girl with the umbrella in both hands. It connected solidly against the side of her head, and her neck bent sideways and down, causing her head to dangle in a way that no head should. She made incoherent croaking sounds as her head lolled horribly to the side. Katya hit her again, but the umbrella had bent in two from the first strike. She dropped it and ran for the back door. As she was reaching for the handle, the girl appeared suddenly in front of it, her head still dangling to the side. She reached to Katya with both hands. Guttural gurgling sounds rose up from her throat.

Katya screamed again, jumped back, turned to the right, and ran up the alley for the front door. Not that it would help, since her key was inside the house. Along with her phone. She didn't get far enough to worry about that, though, as the pale spectre appeared in front of her again.

Katya froze. The girl's neck slowly twisted back into place. Katya could hear the sickening sound of bones crunching against each other as the head repositioned itself. It opened its mouth and dry, choking sounds came out. Katya turned to run back down the alley but the thing appeared before her once again.

Katya dropped to her knees, her hand to her chest. She moaned and began to cry.

"Why would you do that to me?" said the girl.

"I'm sorry," Katya said, through the tears and the rain, not daring to make eye contact with the hideous holes in her attacker's face. "I didn't know. I didn't know it was your heart. The doctors gave it to me."

"But why would you hit me with your umbrella?" said the girl. "Why did you break my neck?"

"Please don't kill me," said Katya, still looking at the ground and crying. "I didn't know. I didn't know it was yours. Don't kill me, please."

The girl frowned and straightened up a bit. "Why would I want to kill you?"

Katya, confused, looked up at the girl. "To... to get your heart back?"

"Why would I want my heart back?" the girl asked. "I don't need it anymore."

Katya blinked up at the girl and squinted, rain falling into her eyes. "Then... then why are you here?"

"I..." the girl began. She choked and gagged like she

was pulling something up her throat from deep inside her. She opened her mouth and a clot of mud and stones dropped out onto the alleyway ground. She coughed and drooled out more mud.

When she spoke again, her voice was considerably less aggressive sounding.

"I just wanted to meet you," she said.

Six

Katya and the dead girl sat on the sofa, listening to music on Katya's laptop. After a long, hot shower, a change of clothes, and a serious hair brushing, she was looking much better. Not that she could feel the heat of the shower, but standing in mist for a while seemed somehow appropriate. A pair of cheap sunglasses completed the illusion of normalcy.

"Anything?" Katya asked her.

The song playing was an aggressively cheerful, boppy number with an autotuned woman singing about nothing in particular. Or maybe about love. Or dancing. It was unclear. It was a very well produced, exceedingly catchy bit of ephemera.

"Nope," said the girl, shaking her head.

"This is the biggest song in the world right now," said Katya. "You must have heard it."

"Maybe? It depends on how long I've been dead."

"Well, it can't have been that long," Katya said. "I mean, I'm not a coroner or anything, but there isn't any decay at all, as far as I can tell."

"Maybe I'm full of formaldehyde or something," said the girl.

"Do they still do that?"

"I have no idea," the girl said. "But I had to have died before you had your transplant, right?"

"I would have thought so but... you know," she said, gesturing vaguely toward the girl. "I'm questioning a lot of my long-held assumptions right now."

"You too, huh?"

"Yeah."

"Funny, that."

One side of Katya's mouth turned down and she made a pensive noise. "Well, my incident was almost three months ago, so maybe we should try something a bit older than that," she said, and she put on a different, but essentially identical song.

"What about this one?" They listened to it for a bit and the girl shook her head. "Just wait for the chorus," Katya said. The chorus happened and the girl shook her head again.

"Nope," she said. "Sorry."

"Maybe you just weren't into music."

"Maybe. I mean, I'm pretty sure I was, but I have nothing to base that on."

"You could have been a Mennonite," Katya said. "There's a community not far from here. Maybe you only listened to Mennonite music."

"Do Mennonites even have music?"

"You know, I'm not sure," said Katya. "If they do, it probably doesn't have a lot of drum machines."

"Yeah," said the girl. "And do they go in for organ donation?"

"I honestly don't know." Katya stopped the song and said, "Maybe we're going about this the wrong way."

"How do you mean?"

"I think I read a thing once that said that smell memories are the strongest. Hang on."

Katya looked around for something smelly. She grabbed a vanilla-scented candle and handed it to the girl, who gave it a sniff.

"Anything?"

"It's nice."

"No memories, though?"

The girl shook her head.

"Okay, hang on," Katya said. She got up, went to the kitchen, and rooted through the fridge. She returned with a foil delivery container with a few scraps of butter chicken. "Try this."

"Mmmm, that smells great."

"Anything?"

"Maybe," said the girl. "I definitely know I like butter chicken."

"How do you know? Are you remembering something?"

"No, it's just that everybody loves butter chicken."

"Not Vijay. But otherwise that's a good point," said Katya, nodding. As she put the chicken back in the fridge, she had an idea. "We should start a mind map."

"A what?"

"A mind map. A bunch of notes full of facts and ideas and whatnot," she said. "Like on cop shows when they put everything they know on a big white board and study it, hoping for connections."

"Sure, I guess."

"Let me find some Post-Its."

Twenty minutes later, the living room wall was covered in little yellow pieces of paper reading things like, *Dead*, *Gravelly Voice*, *Heart Transplant*, and *Mennonite?*

A key sounded in the front door. "Oh, Vijay's home,"

Katya said.

The girl stood awkwardly, unsure of what to do. Katya went to the front hallway and kissed Vijay as he came in the door.

"How are you feeling?" he asked, handing her a small bouquet.

"Oh, wow, thank you," she said, smiling and accepting the flowers. "I'm feeling a bit better. Tired, though. It's been an interesting day."

"Good interesting or bad interesting?" he asked as he sat to untie his shoes.

"A little from column A, and a little from column B," Katya said. "How was the trip?"

"Mostly a waste of time."

"I'm sorry to hear that," Katya said.

"Meh. If they wanna pay me all that overtime to take a trip to Montreal," he said, standing up, "I say let them."

"That certainly works for me."

Vijay walked into the living room and stopped when he saw the girl. "Oh, hello," he said.

"Hi," she said, holding out her hand. "You must be Vijay."

"That's right," said Vijay, being briefly distracted by the sticky notes on the wall. His attention snapped back when he touched her hand. "Oh, you're really cold. Do you want me to turn up the thermostat?"

"It won't help," she said, looking at the flowers.

"Honey, this is my new friend," Katya said.

"Hi. Uh... Sorry, what's your name?"

"That's what we're trying to figure out," said the girl. She leaned towards Katya and smelled the arrangement. "Those are familiar."

"I'm sorry?" Vijay said.

"It's hard to explain," said Katya. "And you're not

going to believe it."

"Okay. Try me," Vijay said. "I try to believe six impossible things every day before breakfast."

"Then crack open an entire dozen eggs because this one's a doozy," Katya said. "Why don't you sit down?"

Vijay plunked himself down in the recliner.

Katya nodded to the girl and said, "Show him."

She unbuttoned the top two buttons of the blouse she was wearing. It occurred to Vijay that his birthday was coming up soon, and he wondered if Katya had found him an early present. He kept a poker face.

The girl opened the blouse just enough to show her scar.

"Oh, you've had the same procedure."

"Kind of," said the girl.

"Except in reverse," Katya said, taking the flowers into the kitchen.

"How do you mean?"

"She's my donor," Katya said, removing a vase from a cupboard.

"I'm sorry?"

"She has my heart," said the girl. "Well, my ex-heart. I don't need it any more."

"Wait, what?" said Vijay.

"It's true," Katya said.

"So whose heart do you have?" Vijay asked the girl.

"Nobody's."

"What, did you get, like, a mechanical one or something? Why would they replace it? Is there something wrong with it?" He jumped out of the chair and bounded to the kitchen doorway. "Is it faulty? Did they give you a faulty heart?"

"No, no, it's fine," Katya said. "It's working great."

"So why isn't it in her?" he said, pointing at the girl.

"Because I don't need it," she said, as Katya pushed

past Vijay, carrying the vase into the living room.

"But..."

"Vijay, I know this is going to sound crazy but... You're going to want to sit down again."

Vijay sat as Katya put the vase on an end table. "Go on," he said.

"She's dead," said Katya.

Vijay stared at Katya in silence for two blinks. "She's what?"

"Dead. She's dead. She died and they gave me her heart."

"Technically I'm undead, I think," said the girl.

"Oh, I suppose so," said Katya. "I'm sorry I said that. Is that offensive; calling you dead?"

"I don't know," said the girl, shaking her head. "I don't think so, though. I mean, I'm not bothered by it, but I have no idea if that's the community consensus or whatever."

"Wait, there's a community?" said Katya.

"I have no idea. I'm guessing no, but I mean..." said the girl, shrugging.

"I think I'm going to need a little more explanation, here," said Vijay.

"Can you show him your eyes?" said Katya.

"You sure? I can understand where the whole eye situation is a bit disturbing."

"I mean, if it's okay with you," said Katya.

"Yeah, I'm fine with it," said the girl.

"What about your eyes?" Vijay asked.

The girl removed her sunglasses to reveal her empty, black eye sockets.

"WHAT THE—" said Vijay, leaning back. "Oh, Jesus. Is this Amar's work?" He leaned forward to examine the eye sockets. "He's getting really good. How did he do that? It looks incredible."

"It's not a special effect, Vijay," said Katya.

"How long were you sitting here like that waiting for me?" Vijay asked. "I mean, he must have done that before coming to the airport to pick me up. I can't believe he kept a straight face the entire time. I can usually tell when he's about to pull some crap on me."

"Vijay," said Katya. "It's not a special effect."

"Sure it isn't."

The girl put her sunglasses back on, looked at Katya, and shrugged. "Should I try that other thing?"

"Yeah, go for it, I guess."

Vijay felt a sudden wind flow past him to fill the space where the girl had just been. A paper blew off of the coffee table. Katya's hair flowed slightly in the breeze.

The clothes she had borrowed from Katya, now suddenly empty, fell to the floor. Katya grabbed the sunglasses on their way down.

"How's that?" came the girl's voice from the kitchen.

"What the—?" said Vijay.

"One second," she said. Vijay and Katya heard the sound of the clothes dryer opening and closing in the basement, then Vijay felt another wind, this one at his back. The girl leaned forward from behind him and put her face beside his.

"Boo!" she said. Vijay jumped out of his chair.

She disappeared, resulting in a wind going in the opposite direction, the air filling the space where she had been. Another wind accompanied her reappearing where she had started, now wearing her funereal dress.

"What—" said Vijay. "How—"

"No idea," said the girl. "Isn't it awesome?"

"You... But... There are mirrors or something, right?"

"Nope."

"A body double? Are you twins?"

"Nope."

"Did you drug me? Am I hallucinating this?"
"Nope."
"Then how... I mean..."
"Do the other thing," said Katya.
"Really?"
"Yeah."
"What other thing?" Vijay asked.
"This," said the girl, and she knocked her neck out of joint.

"Oh, Jesus Christ!" said Vijay. "What the—How are you—"

"We don't know," said the girl, straightening her neck back into a shape more associated with living people, to the sound of neck bones crunching. "The best I can figure is I died of a broken neck."

"But..."

"We only know she can do that because I hit her with an umbrella," said Katya.

"You should have seen the look on her face," the girl said.

Katya laughed. "Oh my God, I was so terrified."

"I'm sorry," said the girl. "I was still pretty out of it at the time. I didn't really know what I was doing."

"I need to sit down," Vijay said, and he lowered himself back into the recliner. Katya and her new friend took their previous places on the sofa. "Katya, this is too weird. You've had your fun at my expense. Whatever's going on, you need to explain it now. Please."

"It's seriously not a joke," said Katya. "A couple of hours ago, I wouldn't have believed it either but, well... I do now."

Vijay stared at Katya open-mouthed for a moment and then turned to the girl. "So... you're dead."

"Yes."

"Undead," said Katya. "Right?"

The girl shrugged. "I guess."

"And this is not a joke."

"No," said Katya.

"And you don't know how you died."

"Right," said the girl.

"Or who you were."

"No."

"Can you remember anything?"

"Not really," she said. "I mean, I can speak, obviously. So remember how to do that. And I can walk. And I can remember a few things like some celebrities. Like, I might not be able to think of them right now, but Katya mentioned Jason Momoa and I remembered him immediately, but I couldn't tell you what he was in."

"She remembers Jason Momoa," Katya said, putting on a husky voice and waggling her eyebrows saucily.

"You all remember Jason Momoa," said Vijay, rolling his eyes.

"But I don't do automatic things like breathing or circulating blood. I guess I don't need to anymore."

"So what's the first thing you *do* remember?" Vijay asked.

"Being cold. And confined," she said.

"You were confined?"

"Well, I was buried," she said. "Did you know the weight of the dirt makes coffins collapse?"

"I did not," said Vijay, attempting and failing to not let his inner reaction to that show on his face.

"I did," said Katya. "I saw it on Mythbusters."

"Mythbusters?" said the girl. "Guy with the big moustache, right? And the other guy."

"You remember it?"

"Maybe? Was there an exploding cement truck?"

"Yes!" said Katya.

"Okay, so there's a new thing I remember," said the girl. "Cool."

"So you remember Mythbusters and being in a collapsed coffin," Vijay said.

"Yeah. Of course, I had no idea where I was," she said. "I just had this overwhelming desire to get out."

"I should think so," Vijay said.

"Were you scared?" Katya asked.

"No. I don't think I had enough awareness of the situation for it to occur to me to be scared," she said. "So I just kind of wiggled my fingers until they moved enough that I could push my hand up, and so on until I dragged myself out of the grave. Then I walked here."

"You walked?" Vijay said. "You didn't just... appear?"

"No," she said, shaking her head. "I don't think I can travel like that to places I've never been."

"I guess that makes sense," said Vijay. "As much as any of this does."

"How long a walk was it?" Katya asked.

"I'm not sure. I think the sun was just going down when I pulled myself out of the ground. And I don't think I walked an entire night and day. No, wait, maybe I did. I remember hiding in a bush. I think. I'm not sure. It's all really fuzzy."

"How did you know where to go?" Vijay asked.

"I don't know," she said. "It wasn't a conscious decision. It was like instinct, I guess. And it just sort of led me here."

"To scare the crap out of me," said Katya.

"Aww, I'm so sorry!"

"It's okay," said Katya, laughing. Then to Vijay she said, "You should have heard her voice. It sounded like gravel."

"Well, I hadn't spoken for probably three months. And there was actual, literal gravel in my throat."

"Seriously, though, it was so creepy," said Katya.

"Like Tom Waites gargling drain cleaner," said the girl.

"Wait, you know who Tom Waites is?" Vijay said.

"Huh," said the girl, frowning slightly. "I suppose I do. Now. Neat."

"What about that teleportation thing?" Vijay asked. "How do you do that?"

"I don't know. I just do," she said. "I think about it and there I am."

"Like a blink dog," Vijay said. They both looked at him quizzically. "Like in Dungeons and Dragons. They're these dogs that just kind of blink and appear somewhere else."

"Sounds right. Maybe I'm part blink dog," said the girl.

"And the thing with the clothes?" he said, gesturing to the pile on the floor.

"It seems like I can't teleport or whatever with anything I wasn't buried with," she said. "Which basically means my dress and that's it."

"Is it dry, by the way?" said Katya.

"Yeah, it's fine."

"Do you have other... powers?" Vijay asked.

"Powers?" Katya asked. "Really?"

"Well, what do you call them?" Vijay asked.

"I don't know. Not powers. That's some comic book shit."

"She's undead. She can blink around all over the place," said Vijay. "Those sound like powers to me."

"It just sounds weird," Katya said. "I should probably add it to the wall, though," and she grabbed the sticky notes.

"I don't mind," the girl said. "It's kind of cool. I always wanted superpowers."

"Really?" Katya asked. "Are you remembering something?"

"No, I just assume. I mean, who wouldn't want superpowers?"

"That's a valid point," Katya said, nodding. "They're like the butter chicken of the supernatural."

She added *Superpowers* as a heading on a sticky note and put it on the wall. Under that, she put *Blink Travel*.

"Can you fly?" Vijay asked.

"I don't think so."

"Move faster than a speeding bullet?"

"Not really, but I think the blink dog thing kind of covers that."

"Can you spin a web? Any size?"

She made the web-shooting motion with her wrist. Nothing happened. "Nope."

"Heat vision?"

She stared at a blank spot on the wall and concentrated. Nothing combusted. "Nope."

"What about, like, super hearing or fire breath or clairvoyance?"

"No, none of that," she said. "Just the blinking thing, I think. And the ability to see without eyes."

"Yeah, that one is pretty cool, I guess."

"And the heart-finding thing," said Katya.

"Cardiovascular Geopositioning," said the girl.

"Is that a thing?" Vijay asked.

"It is now," she said.

"That's a good one," Katya said, adding it under *Superpowers*.

"Can you walk on water?" Vijay asked.

She considered that for a moment and said, "I don't know. I think I remember a bridge on my walk but no actual water. There might have been a creek but I'm not sure."

Five minutes later they were in the washroom, the tub filling with water.

"That's probably enough," said the girl. "I only need an inch or so."

"Okay," said Katya, turning off the water. The girl stepped into the bath and failed to not sink.

"Nope," she said.

"Do you need to eat?" Vijay asked.

"I don't think so," she said. "I'm pretty sure I haven't eaten since I woke up and I'm not hungry. Although that food smelled good. So maybe I can but don't actually need to?"

"I wonder what happens when you drink alcohol," Vijay said.

"No idea," she said, shrugging.

"Well, there's only one way to find out."

"Shore Leave?" Katya asked.

"Shore Leave," Vijay agreed.

"What's Shore Leave?"

Seven

Shore Leave was Port Langston's best and only tiki bar.

Roy and Julia, the bar's rockabilly-loving owners, had misspent their youths in punk bands, tattoo shops, and roller derby leagues before settling down in a sprawling Port Langston century home inherited from Julia's family. They had spared no expense at several dollar stores gathering decorations for their labor of love. Coconut monkeys, shell bras, mermaid-based black velvet paintings, rubber sharks, wobbly hula girls, and bamboo everything were the order of the day.

The weekday soundtrack was pure Exotica; a short-lived musical genre from the late nineteen-fifties. A sort of ersatz World Music from a time before a composer could research the traditional music of far-off lands with a few clicks of a button. It was all made up and, of course, entirely inaccurate. But that didn't stop it from being inventive and entirely unique for its time.

Weekends were a different story, when Roy and Julia

let their hair down and relaxed the rules of authentic Tiki culture, trading in Les Baxter and Elizabeth Waldo for Motorhead and The Clash.

This being a Monday, however, Katya, Vijay, and the girl were treated to the sounds of marimba and vibraphone pretending to be the sounds of the some South Pacific island as they made their way past the smokers outside and up to the door, where they nodded to the bouncer.

"Clark," said Vijay.

Clark was six-foot-four and apparently made of tattoos in a black t-shirt.

"Vij," said Clark, nodding back. "Kitty Kat. It's been way too long. How are you feeling?"

"Heya, Clark," Katya said. "I'm on the mend and in need of a drink."

"Well, you've come to the right place," he said, stepping back from the door.

"Glad to hear it," Katya said, squeezing past him and into the bar.

"Hang on. Who's your friend?"

"This is my niece, Mary," Katya said. "She's come from Boston to visit for a bit."

"She old enough to be in here?"

"Of course she is," Katya said. "You don't think I'd take an underage niece out drinking, do you? My sister would have my hide."

"You might. Vijay wouldn't, though. Too much of a pussy," he said, grinning.

"I'd never risk getting banned from the only bar in town my wife is still allowed to drink at."

"Night's young," said Clark.

"Challenge accepted," Katya said.

"You'll do your best, I'm sure," said Clark.

"Always do," said Katya.

"Sunglasses at night, huh?" Clark said to the girl.

"They're prescription," she said. "My pupils don't shrink. They're permanently dilated."

"Mydriasis," Clark said. "My cousin's got that. Like Bowie."

"Exactly."

"All right, well, you have a good night."

"Thanks," she said, and followed Katya.

"I'm like Bowie," the girl said to Katya in a look-how-impressive-I-am sort of way.

The bar was surprisingly full for a Monday night, but they found a reasonably secluded table in a corner under a photo of Elvis from "Blue Hawaii" and settled in. The table only wobbled slightly, and it was early enough in the night that it wasn't sticky.

"Quick thinking with the medical issue there... *Mary*," Vijay said.

"Thanks. Speaking of... Mary?"

"It was the first name that popped into my mind."

"Do you actually have a niece named Mary?" the girl asked.

"No, I'm an only child."

"That explains the lamest name ever," said the girl.

"Well, what do you want to be called?"

"By my actual name."

"Which is...?"

She pondered for a moment and said, "Yeah, I have no idea."

"Damn. I was hoping it'd just come to you subconsciously."

"Yeah, I figured," the girl said. "That's why it didn't work."

"Okay, I'm going to find some drinks," said Vijay. "Who wants what?"

"Jet pilot," said Katya.

"Jesus, you're starting the night out hard, are you? Am I going to have to carry you home?"

"It's a distinct possibility," said Katya.

"And you?" he asked the girl.

"Surprise me, I guess."

"Any allergies?"

"Bananas."

Katya and Vijay stared at her for a moment, expectantly.

"Oh!" She smiled and perked up. "Bananas! I'm allergic to bananas! That's a thing I know now."

"How do you know?" Katya asked.

"I don't know. It was just… there."

"Okay, so one jet pilot and one something without bananas," Vijay said, and he headed to the bar.

"So let's get back to this name situation," said the girl. "I can't be a Mary."

"What would you like it to be?"

"I don't know. Something cool. Leia? Princess Awesome Pants? Poopalaka, Queen of the Undead Hordes?"

"I don't see any hordes. Just you."

"The night is young," said Maybe-Poopalaka.

"What about Sarah?"

"Sarah?" she said, wrinkling her nose.

"What's wrong with Sarah?"

"It's just so basic. It's the name parents give to their fourth daughter, when all the good names are taken and they just don't care anymore."

"Okay, so not Sarah."

"It's like a default ringtone," said Unsarah. "Like that standard Windows background wallpaper. It's the cheese pizza of names, you know? Like, sure it's serviceable, but it's just kinda there."

"Okay, so you want your name to be a Meat Lovers,"

said Katya.

"Sure. Or something with Gouda and chorizo. Maybe a hand-made wood-fired deal."

"Well, aren't we pan-European?" said Katya. "So something Dutch and Spanish? Maybe you can be Lotte Matute."

"You're on the right track."

"Sofia Rasmussen?"

"That's pretty cool, but it doesn't feel like me," she said.

"What about Cynthia?"

"That's a crazy girl's name."

"Well, I mean, the jury's out until we know more about you."

"Fair. But I don't think I feel like a Cynthia," she said. "I feel like I'll know my name when I hear it. Maybe."

"That's not a lot to go on," Katya said. "And we can't just go on calling you 'Hey, You!'"

"It could make the Name Game awkward."

"Oh, I know!" said Katya. "Bela."

"Bella was the human. The vampire was Edward."

"I was thinking Lugosi," said Katya, as Vijay returned with drinks. "Also, how do you know that?"

"Once again, I have no idea," she said.

Vijay set a tall, colorful beverage on the table in front of the girl.

"Ooh, what's this?" she asked.

"A zombie," he said, suppressing a grin.

"Dude!" said Katya, receiving her jet pilot. Vijay sat down with his lager.

"Nice," said Possibly-Bela. "Liquid cannibalism."

"You're not a zombie, though," Katya said. "You would have eaten our brains by now."

"True. I guess."

"I wonder what you actually are, then," said Vijay. "I

mean, you're not a vampire, right? Can you go outside in the daytime?"

"I think so. But that doesn't necessarily rule out vampirism," she said. "Dracula could go out in the daytime. Vampires weren't sensitive to sunlight until the movie *Nosferatu* in 1922."

"So you can remember that but not who you are," said Vijay as she took a sip of her zombie.

"Apparently. I mean, it's not like I was just sitting there on that information," she said. "It just sort of came to me when you mentioned vampires and sunlight."

"Right, no, I get that," he said. "It's just bizarre which memories come back and which ones don't."

"Brains are weird, I guess."

"As long as they're not delicious," said Vijay.

"I don't plan on finding out," she said.

"You'd starve to death on this one anyway," said Katya, tilting her head in Vijay's direction.

"Hey! I... No, she's right."

"I can't think of any undead creatures that can blink," said Katya. "Or even move really fast."

"They're not known for their speed, are they?" said the girl.

"Not for the most part, no," said Vijay. "Except newer zombies, which I don't really care for. I wish I still had my old Monster Manual."

They sat in silence for a moment. Vijay pointed at the girl and said, "Nancy Wilson."

"What?"

"That's your name."

They both stared at him, expectantly.

"The guitarist from Heart," he said.

The women looked at each other, each with a raised eyebrow.

"No? Okay, how about Bret?" said Vijay.

"Bret?" asked Definitely-Not-Bret.

"As in Bret 'The Hitman' Hart?" said Katya.

"Exactly," he said. "That's what I'm calling you from now on. The Hitman. Or just Hitman for short."

"You are not calling her Hitman," Katya said.

"Honestly, it's better than Sarah," she said.

"Melissa Joan," said Katya excitedly.

"A heart-based name which has the added benefit of being a Teenage Witch," said Vijay.

"Oh, I hadn't even thought of that," said Katya. "Actually, Sabrina's an okay name."

"That's not terrible," said the girl. "I mean, as a placeholder."

"Sabrina's not undead, though," Vijay said.

"Well, we can't have everything, can we?" said Maybe Sabrina.

"Nope, I've got it," Vijay said. "I know what we're calling you."

"Hit it," she said.

"Hearty Farty The Funeral Party."

"Wow," said the young lady who was definitely not named that.

"How many of those have you had?" said Katya, gesturing to Vijay's beer.

"Like four sips," said Vijay.

"You do realize that you are absolutely forbidden from naming so much as a pet from now on, yes?"

"That's probably a good idea," he said, looking at a plate of wings being carried past. "I should have grabbed a snack menu. Be right back," and off he went.

"How's the zombie?" Katya asked.

Not-Hearty-Farty wrinkled her nose and said, "I can't really taste it."

"No?"

"Not really. I mean, it's like I know what it tastes like and I know it's cold but I can't actually experience it. If that makes sense."

"Not really."

Katya was about to go back to asking about music and TV shows to see if anything would trigger a memory when cloud of cheap body spray with some guy inside it grabbed Vijay's chair, turned it around, and sat on it backwards. He wore a white baseball hat at an angle and a too-tight, striped, short-sleeve polo shirt.

"'Sup, ladies?" he said.

"No," said Katya.

"Having a good night?"

"Dude?" Katya said. "Not interested. Please just move along."

"Sunglasses inside, huh?" he said, turning to Melissa-For-Now. "That's cool. I can dig that."

"She's not interested," Katya said. "We're trying to have a discussion here."

"Oh, she's interested," he said. "I can tell she's interested. Aren't you?"

"I'm really not," she said.

"Sure you are. You just don't know it yet."

She leaned in towards the guy and lowered her sunglasses so he could see the black pits where her eyes used to be. His mouth fell open and he jerked backwards.

The girl spoke with a voice that sounded like shattered, filthy gravel grinding against vocal cords made of glass. The voice said, "AROINT THEE, MOTHERFUCKER, BACK TO THE JIZZ-ENCRUSTED SHITHOLE FROM WHENCE YOU CAME!"

The guy's eyes widened, as did Katya's, and he nearly fell backwards off his chair.

"Holy shit!" he said, backing up. "Jesus!"

"HE'S NOT HERE," she said.

"I was just trying to be friendly," said the guy, backing away. "Crazy bitch."

He backed into another patron, spun around and glared at them, and disappeared into the crowd, muttering.

"Holy crap," said Katya as Vijay returned.

"What was that all about?" he said.

"I think Sabrina here found another superpower."

"That? That's just a death metal growl," she said. "I learned it from YouTube tutorials."

"Death metal?"

"Yeah, I love metal," she said. "Oh my God! I just remembered! I love metal!"

"I had a Poison album in high school," said Katya.

"No, not hair metal," she said. "The good stuff. Napalm Death. Slayer. The Agonist."

"Maybe that's why you came back," said Vijay. "You made a deal with Satan."

"Seriously?" she said. "Right now, there's a person in another city rolling their eyes and they don't know why. You ever listen to Voivod?"

"Who?" said Katya.

"That's got to be why none of your music triggered any memories," said Placeholder Sabrina. "It's garbage."

"Hey!"

"Sorry but it's kind of true."

"She's not wrong," said Vijay.

"So how did you get into that kind of stuff?" Katya asked.

"My older brother, Jarred. He was into that stuff and got me into it," she said. Then she looked downwards. "Oh my God, Jarred." She tilted her head back up again. "I have a brother named Jarred. He's in a band. When I was little I used to laugh at him for it. I learned to do the voice so I could make fun of him but then I got into it."

"Jarred," said Katya, nodding. "That's great. What else do you remember about him?"

"He took me to my first concert," she said. "I wasn't old enough but he knew the promoter from his own band, so he let me in as long as I pretended to be working the merch table. We went to see Arch Enemy and Nightwish."

"That's great," said Katya.

"We never told my parents," she said. "I wonder if they ever found out."

"Tell me about your parents," said Katya.

Not-Sabrina opened her mouth as if to speak, but nothing came out. She frowned and closed her mouth and looked away. "I... no. Nothing. They're like shadows just outside of my peripheral. Like, I know I had them. But I can't remember anything." She set her drink down, sat back, and stared into the distance. "Jarred, though. I miss him."

"We'll find him," said Katya. "We'll find him and explain what happened and you'll go to lots more concerts."

"Yeah," she said. "I hope so."

"We'll do everything we can to help," said Katya. "Right, Vijay?"

"Yes, of course," he said. "Whatever you need."

"Thanks. Seriously, thank you so much. I'm glad I've found you two," she said. "You'd have every reason to be scared of me. I wouldn't have blamed you if you'd taken me out with a shovel. Or if you'd called the cops or the army or had scientists dissect me or to sell me to some crazy billionaire as a medical freak show for his collection of oddities. But no. Instead, you take me out drinking and help me remember who I am. That's seriously cool. Thank you."

"You didn't tell her about the crazy billionaire?" said Katya.

"I thought you were going to break it to her."

"I knew it was too good to last," the girl said.

"It's just that I've had my eye on this really cool Jet-Ski," said Vijay.

"And an oceanfront mansion to park it beside," said Katya.

"That's fair," she said, nodding. "I mean, who wouldn't trade someone's life for a Jet-Ski?"

"And a mansion," said Katya.

"Afterlife, technically," said Vijay. They both looked at him. "I just made it kind of weird, didn't I?"

"Oh, I'm pretty sure it got weird the moment I showed up."

"I can't argue that," Katya said.

"I'm starting to think weird isn't a new thing for you," said Vijay.

Forty minutes and another beer and zombie later, Vijay asked if the drinks were affecting her.

"Nah," she said, shaking her head. "They do want out, though. Where are the washrooms in this place?"

"Downstairs," Vijay said, pointing. "Beside the entrance."

"Cool, thanks," she said and she weaved her way through the crowd to the front. She nodded to Clark on the way past and stepped through the doorway to the stairs. She began to take her first step down when she was hit with a sudden dizzy spell. The stairs seemed to widen and shrink nauseatingly. A memory flooded back to her of another stairway, one much wider and with lush carpeting. It curved around and to the right. An ornate banister led downwards to end in front of a massive double door under a chandelier. She saw the staircase rushing up to meet her. Her foot slipped. She grabbed the handrail and yelped.

"Whoa," said Clark, rushing over to steady her. "You okay?"

She stammered, stepped backwards, and sank to her knees.

"Nope, you can't sit there," Clark said. "This is a thoroughfare."

She steadied herself against the wall with one hand and put the other on the floor.

"Sorry, but I've got to ask you to leave."

"What?"

"You're inebriated," said Clark. "You've got to go. Come on."

He helped her up and led her to a chair by the entrance. "Hang on, I'll get Vij and Kat," he said, and disappeared into the crowd.

He reappeared a few moments later with Katya in tow. "What happened?" she asked.

"I just had a dizzy spell."

"I'm sorry, Kat," Clark said. "She can't stay here."

"She's not drunk, I promise."

"Maybe not, but I can't risk it. The cops have been super crazy with us lately. If she needs medical attention, I can call an ambulance. Or get her a ride to Emergency."

Katya momentarily considered the hubbub that taking a walking dead person to the hospital would cause and thought better of it. "No, no. That's cool. We've got her." Then she held out her hand to the girl and said, "Shall we?"

"Sure. Wait, where's Vijay?"

"He's just taking care of the bill."

"Sorry, Kat, I've gotta," said Clark. "You understand.

We can't afford to lose our license."

"No, of course not," Katya said. "It's fine."

She and the girl stepped out of the bar, navigated the gaggle of smokers, and awaited Vijay on the sidewalk. He caught up to them and asked what happened.

"I fell down the stairs," said the girl.

"Are you okay?"

"I thought you just slipped a bit," Katya said.

"No, I mean before. That's how I died."

"Are you sure?" Vijay asked.

"I'm positive," she said. "I saw it clear as day. I fell down this big, ornate staircase and broke my neck."

"That would explain that... thing you can do," said Katya. "With your head."

"I suppose it would," she said, nodding. "And the viability of my organs. And the bruises."

"Bruises?" Vijay asked. "What bruises?"

She pulled up her sleeve to reveal an oddly-shaped black patch. "I've got the same on both knees and my one leg."

"You do?" he said. "I'm surprised I didn't notice them when you were demonstrating your blinking thing."

"I think you were kind of preoccupied with the whole there's-a-dead-girl-in-my-house situation," the girl said.

"Yeah, that's true," he said.

"I noticed them when we were getting you cleaned up," said Katya. "But I didn't want to say anything. Just in case... well, I don't know."

"Yeah, I get it," the girl said.

"So we just have to find references to a girl who fell down the stairs and had a brother named Jarred," Vijay said, pulling out his phone. He searched as they walked but it came up empty.

They continued home, passing by the various shops found in the outskirt neighbourhoods of any town; convenience stores, restaurants, accountants and more. They varied from small, family-owned shops to small versions of giant national chains. At one point, they passed a florist.

"Hey, flowers," said the girl, stopping to look through the window. "I like flowers. I'm pretty sure."

"Most people do, I think," Katya said.

"Yeah, but... it seems like more than that. Like, I know without looking that that one there," she said, pointing to a delicate white orchid with slender green leaves, "...is a Dendobium. And that one beside it is a Lily of the Incas. Why do I know that?"

"I don't know," said Katya. "But that bouquet Vijay brought home triggered something, too."

"It did, didn't it? So that's definitely a thing," she said. "It's like it's sitting on the tip of my brain."

"Maybe we should call you Lily," said Vijay. "Or Daisy."

"I thought I was Hearty Farty."

"Well, you know," said Vijay. "A rose by any other name..."

The girl straightened up suddenly and turned away from the window to face him. "That's it!" she said. "I've heard that before."

"It's Shakespeare," Katya said.

"No, besides that. It's the shop."

"What shop?" Katya asked.

"The flower shop," she said. "By Any Other Name. I can see it, clear as day. I know that place. It means something."

Vijay pulled out his phone again and searched. "Yep, there's a florist by that name in Hackett."

"Can we go?" she said.

"Of course."

"Right now? I need to see it."

"It'll be closed right now, I'm sure," Katya said. "But we can go tomorrow."

"When will you get home from work?"

"Forget work," she said. "I'll call in. I'll tell them today was too stressful and I need another day."

"I mean, you're not wrong," said the girl.

"All I know is I'm gonna laugh so hard if your name turns out to be Sarah," Vijay said.

Eight

The next morning found Katya and her new friend parked outside By Any Other Name, a florist in downtown Port Hackett. It was small and a bit run down, but the window was filled with colourful floral displays offering suggestions for any potential upcoming birthdays or anniversaries. The sign was cracked and one of the lights behind it was out.

The girl was sitting low in the passenger seat, her feet against the glove compartment, knees pulled up against her chest. She wore a frayed, grey hoodie and her usual sunglasses. Her hair was tucked up into a black baseball hat.

"I can't go in," she said.

"I'm sure they'd love to see you."

"Maybe," she said. "Or maybe not. I don't know yet."

"Yeah, that's a fair point," said Katya. "Okay, I'm going in."

Katya left the car and went into the store. It was warm and smelled of dirt and pollen. Gorgeous floral arrangements surrounded her. A woman in her early fifties stood behind the counter, speaking with a man buying an anniversary arrangement.

Katya wandered around the shop. It was clean and the arrangements were beautiful, but the place needed a new paint job and the floors were well-worn. She admired the displays and looked for any sort of clue. And then she spotted one. Behind the counter, sitting on a shelf, was a photo of three people standing outside the store on a beautiful, sunny day. The store in the photo looked brighter and fresher. In the middle was the woman behind the counter. To either side were two kids. One, a long-haired young man wearing a black shirt with an unreadable band logo. The other was the girl. She was a few years younger and still had her eyes, but it was her.

This was definitely the right place.

The man left with his arrangement and the woman turned to Katya. "Hi, how are you?"

"I'm great. How are you doing?"

"Can't complain. What can I help you with?"

"To be honest, I'm just killing time waiting for a friend."

"Oh, well that's fine."

"Great store you have here," said Katya.

"Thanks. I'm pretty proud of it."

"You should be. Do you own the place?"

"I do," said the woman. "Nearly fifteen years now."

"Oh, that's great," Katya said. "I've driven past this place so many times but I've never been in. It's very comfy. Kind of homey."

"Good, that's what I was going for," the woman said. "I spend so much time here I want it to be a pleasant environment. Plus I think customers like it."

"Well, I know I do," Katya said, smiling. She gestured to the photo. "A family arrangement?"

"Yes. Well, it was," she said. "The kids are grown now but they used to help out a lot. Jarred just moved to Boston for a job."

"Oh, good for him," said Katya, genuinely happy for Jarred. "And that's your daughter?"

"Rose," she said, looking away.

"Rose," Katya repeated. "A fitting name. What does she do?"

"She, um... well... She's no longer with us."

"Oh," said Katya.

"Yeah."

"I'm very sorry," Katya said. "She was so young."

"Barely twenty-three," she said.

"That's awful. Can I ask what happened?"

"Car accident," she said. "A deer ran out on the road one night, and..."

"...she swerved?"

Rose's mom nodded. "She liked animals. She knew better than to swerve for a deer, but..." She stared into the distance, looking at nothing.

"Yeah," said Katya. "But, I mean, we've all done it, right? I know I have."

"I suppose so. At least Bradley was okay. Her boyfriend," she added. "He was in the car with her at the time. It was amazing that he survived."

"That's something, I guess."

"They met right here. He was buying flowers for his mom."

"Sounds like a good guy."

"He was," she agreed. "I haven't seen him since the funeral. I suspect this place would just bring him bad memories."

"That's understandable."

"Sorry," Rose's mom said, coming back to reality. "It's barely been three months so I'm still trying to deal. I don't mean to unload on a stranger."

"It's quite all right. My name is Katya, by the way," she said, offering her hand. "Katya Carter."

"Iris Kaidan," she said, shaking Katya's hand.

"See, now we're not strangers," Katya said. "So it's all good."

Iris grinned. "Thanks for understanding."

"Of course," Katya said. "Things will get better. I promise."

"Thank you."

"But I should go meet my friend. I'll see you again."

"Okay," said Iris. "You have a good day."

Katya went back to the car, sat down and closed the door.

"Your name is Rose."

Rose sat up and looked at Katya, her mouth agape. "Rose Kaidan!"

"Yes. Your mom owns the flower shop."

"Of course she does. She bought it with Dad's life insurance money."

"She didn't mention that."

"I worked there evenings and weekends," said Rose. "So did Jarred. He didn't really like it, though."

"And this all just came flooding back?" said Katya. "Just like that?"

"Just like that," said Rose. "It's like it was always there and I just couldn't access it. Now that I can, the time when I couldn't is starting to feel... wrong. Like a dream. Sort of."

"Well, I'm glad you're making some progress."

"Me too."

"So are you going to go in and talk to her?"

"What?" she said, horrified. "No."

"I'm sure she'd love to know that you're okay."

"I'm not okay," Rose said. "I'm dead. My organs are

gone."

"But you're... You know. Whatever you are. You're here. And I'm sure you'll get more information from her. Maybe just from seeing her."

"No," Rose said, shaking her head. "I can't. It's not fair for her to lose me again. I can't make her go through that twice."

"Who says they will?" Katya said. "You could have years left ahead of you. Hell, you could be immortal. Who knows?"

"I'm not," Rose said. "I don't have a lot of time."

"Why do you say that?"

"Just a feeling."

Katya looked away. She didn't know what to say about that, so she looked straight ahead for a few moments.

"She said you had a boyfriend."

"Did I?"

"Bradley, I think your mom said."

"Oh, yeah. Bradley," she said, nodding. "He wasn't going to be my boyfriend much longer, though."

"I'm sorry to hear that. Your mom seemed to like him."

"Yeah. I did too, at one point. I think," said Rose. "He's still a little vague."

Katya started the car and pulled out onto the street.

"How did you say you died?"

"I fell down the stairs," Rose said. "Broke my neck."

"Huh."

"Why?"

"It's just that your mom said you were in a car accident."

"No," said Rose, looking at her, quizzically. "I definitely fell down the stairs. I remember it clearly."

"I wonder why she said otherwise."

"No idea," she said. "That's weird."

"I guess we've got a lot to add to the wall," Katya said.

Nine

Rose stood looking at the wall. The sticky notes were now accompanied by photos of Iris Kaidan and By Any Other Name that Katya had found on the Internet. In the center were two cards with *Stairs?* and *Car Accident?* scrawled on them. Around them, some joined with little paper arrows, were things like, *Other organs gone? Metal voice*, *Powers*, under which was *Blink/Teleportation*, and *Cardiovascular Geolocation*. To the left was a series of cards listing various undead creatures such as *Zombie*, *Vampire*, *Wight*, and *Ghost*. They were each crossed out with a red "X" and an explanation as to why she wasn't one of them.

Katya stuck up a new card with a description of Rose's bruises on it. She stood back and tried to take in the whole picture, hoping to see a previously-unnoticed connection.

"Wait," she said. "Your bruises."

"What about them?"

"You just have the ones on your legs and arms?"

"Yeah."

"Nothing across your hips or chest?"

"Like a seat belt injury, you mean?"

"Exactly," said Katya. "I was in a fender bender once and I had seat belt bruises for weeks. And if you hadn't been wearing yours, you'd be a lot more messed up than you are."

"I always wear it," Rose said. "And I wasn't in a car accident."

"Then why did your mom say you were?"

"Either she's embarrassed about having a daughter klutzy enough to fall down the stairs or she thinks that's what happened."

"She didn't strike me as the sort to care that much about appearances."

"I think you're probably right," said Rose.

"And there was nothing in the news about you."

"Nope."

"I wonder if we should find your boyfriend and ask him."

"Absolutely not," said Rose.

"Why not?"

"I don't know. It just feels wrong."

"Okay," said Katya. They stood, staring at the Big Board for a while until Katya snapped her fingers. "I know who we can ask."

"Who?"

"Someone who would know what happened but would have no personal attachment to you."

"Who?"

Ten

Dr. Denise Kaylock, the Langston County Coroner, was in her office, where she wore a black pantsuit as opposed to the scrubs she wore while doing what most people would consider the less savoury parts of her job. She sat behind her desk, looking stressed but smiling.

"Thank you so much for seeing me," Katya said, opening a notebook. "I promise I won't take up too much of your time."

"It's no problem at all," said Dr. Kaylock. "Can I ask what your screenplay is about?"

"Well, to some extent I'm still trying to figure that out," Katya said. "What you tell me today will hopefully help me decide."

"I'd love to help you out," she said, folding her hands on the desk. "To be honest, I've always thought it would be a lot of fun to be a consultant for the movies or a cop show."

"That does sound kind of awesome."

"It does," said Dr. Kaylock, nodding. "Most of them

are so removed from reality, they're basically unwatchable to me. It would be great to be involved with one that's hyper realistic. That really takes process and facts seriously."

"That's exactly what I want for my book," Katya said.

"Then bring it on," said the doctor, laughing.

"Fantastic," Katya said with a smile. "So is it true that a person killed in a car accident will have the same bruises as someone who survives one?"

"Well, that depends," said the doctor. "Assuming both hypothetical passengers were identical, physically. The same height, the same weight, and so on. And assuming the crashes were the same. The same vehicles moving at the same speed, with the same safely measure. Then, yes, they would suffer similar injuries."

"Right. So hypothetically, if everything was exactly identical, just that one car was moving just fast enough to cause a fatality and the other wasn't moving quite that fast, they'd still have basically identical seat belt bruises?"

"Assuming they were wearing their seat belts, yes," said Dr. Kaylock. "If they weren't, things get more complex, depending on what happened to them; whether or not they went through the windshield or hit the back of the front seat. And the nature of the accident itself can make a difference."

"But someone who wasn't wearing their seat belt is going to be pretty badly damaged compared to someone who was."

"Probably. But anyone actually killed in a vehicular accident is going to be quite badly injured, seat belt or no seat belt. Of course, much of the damage could be internal."

"That makes sense," said Katya, nodding and

making notes. "But if they were wearing their seat belt and it functioned correctly but they still died, the body would have the same seat belt injuries as someone who survived. Bruising across the hips and in a diagonal along the torso."

"Assuming everything else is identical, yes." said the doctor.

"So if somebody had bruises on their knees, leg, and forearms, but no seat belt marks, and a broken neck, they probably didn't die in a car accident. Correct?"

"That doesn't sound indicative of a collision, no," she said.

"So what would cause injuries like that?"

"Wait, you already know your murder victim's injuries?"

"Yes," said Katya, nodding. "Or I think I do, anyway. I have a lot of character sketches but the plot is still very up in the air."

"I'd be very curious to read it when it's done."

"Actually, that would be amazing," Katya said. "I'd love to have you double-check the science before I send it off."

"I'd be happy to."

"Amazing, thank you. So… what are the chances that someone with the injuries I described died in a car accident while belted in?"

"Slim. If not impossible."

"How slim?" Katya asked.

"Very," said the coroner. "But strange things happen every day. There are so many variants at play in any situation like that. Velocity, weight of the car, safety devices, angle of the impact—"

"So how can you differentiate?" Katya asked.

"Well, that's highly technical," she said. "And it's going to vary from incident to incident."

"So how did you determine the cause of death in the case of Rose Kaidan?"

Dr. Kaylock's eyes widened almost imperceptibly and her head jerked back slightly. "I'm sorry?" she said, coolly.

"Rose Kaidan," Katya repeated. "She died a little over three months ago. You ruled it a vehicular collision but her wounds were more indicative of a fall. How could you tell the difference?"

"I'm sorry, I can't discuss my patients," she said. "Privacy issues."

"They're dead," said Katya. "How much privacy do they need?"

"Again, I'm sorry. But it's the law."

"Oh," Katya said. "Okay. It's just that she was a friend of mine."

"I'm very sorry," said Dr. Kaylock. "You have my sincerest condolences but I just can't give out any information specific to any case."

"Nothing at all?" said Katya. "Even a little, non-specific hint?"

"I could lose my job," Dr. Kaylock said. "In fact, I think it's best if we end this conversation right now."

"I understand," said Katya. "I'm sorry, I didn't intend any offense."

"It's fine," said Dr. Kaylock. "And I'm sorry, as well, but I'm going to have to ask you to leave now."

Without a word, Katya stood and left the office. She walked calmly down the hallway until she turned a corner, at which point she speed-walked to the car.

She got in and closed the door.

"How'd it go?" Rose asked.

"I couldn't get much out of her," said Katya. "But your bruises are not from a car accident. And you should have seen her reaction when I mentioned your name. Yeah, something weird is definitely up."

"To the Big Board?"

"To the Big Board."

Eleven

Early that evening, Vijay arrived home from work and Katya greeted him at the door. "She's got a name," she said.

"Please tell me it's Sarah," he said as Rose walked into the front hallway.

"No such luck."

"Oh my God, it's Hearty Farty, isn't it?"

"That's it," said Rose. "Turns out you were right."

"Awesome."

Katya, grinning, said, "No, no, no... Vijay Mehta, meet Rose Kaidan."

"Rose?"

"Hi," said Rose.

"Seriously? Please tell me you're not kidding," said Vijay. He looked at the confused expressions on their faces. "Rose," he repeated, as if that explained everything.

Rose groaned in comprehension and slumped. "Oh, God. My name is a pun."

"Oh, no," said Katya.

"I'd say 'Kill me,' but... You know."

They settled into the living room as Katya told Vijay all about the day's adventures, from the flower shop to the coroner.

"So something weird is definitely up," he said.

"That's what I said," said Katya.

"I heard her say it," said Rose, nodding.

"So what now?" Vijay asked.

"That's what we're trying to figure out," said Rose.

"We checked the Internet for news about her death but all we got was her obituary," Katya said.

"Not even a mention of the accident?" Vijay asked.

"Nope, nothing," Rose said. "We seem to have come to a standstill."

"I have a suggestion but you're not going to like it," Katya said to Rose.

"What is it?"

"We find your boyfriend."

"I can't," said Rose. "I told you, I can't put anyone through that."

"Well, you don't have to," Katya said. "Leave it up to us."

Rose considered it for a moment and said, "Yeah, I guess. I still can't remember a lot about him, for some reason."

"We could try just driving around Hackett until something looks familiar," Vijay said.

"That sounds time-consuming," said Rose.

"You've got somewhere better to be?"

"No, I suppose not," she said, shrugging. "I can't think of a better plan."

They were interrupted by a knock on the door. Vijay answered it to find a uniformed police officer. At about six-foot-two, he fairly towered over Vijay. He looked to be nearing retirement age, but appeared to be in better shape than most men half his age, even if his midsection had expanded more than he wanted over the last few years. He had the bearing of a man who was used to getting his way and, when he didn't get it immediately, knew how to expedite the matter through intimidation or worse.

"Sheriff Wagner, Langston County P. D.," he said. "I'm looking for a Katya Carter."

"Can I ask what this is about?"

"That's between Miss Carter and I, sir," he said. "Are you a friend of hers?"

"I'm her husband."

"Husband?" he said, sneering. "Then you should know where she is."

"Who is it, honey?" said Katya, coming to the door.

"Katya Carter?" he asked.

"Yes. What can I help you with, Officer?"

"Do you have any identification?"

She briefly considered asking him if she was obligated to do so, but decided that she would be better off not to antagonize him.

"Sure, hang on," she said, and she grabbed her purse and handed over her license. He gave it a cursory glance and handed it back.

"I understand you paid a visit to the coroner's office today," he said.

Hearing this from the other room, Rose backed quietly into the kitchen and stood at the top of the basement stairs, just in case she had to make a quick exit.

"That's right," Katya said.

"Can I ask why?"

"I was looking for some information for a screenplay I'm working on."

"So you're a screenwriter."

"I'm trying to be," she admitted.

"Because I'm given to understand you're a bank teller."

"Loan officer," she said.

"But you're making a movie."

"I'm writing a screenplay," she said. "It involves a death and I want the science to be accurate."

"I'm sure you do," he said. "Dr. Kaylock tells me you were asking about one of her patients in particular."

"Rose Kaidan," she said, nodding. She figured there was no point in trying to bamboozle him beyond what she had already told the coroner. "She was a friend of mine. She kind of helped inspire my story."

"Your story is about a car accident?"

"It's not about it, per se, but there's a car accident in it," she said. "Maybe."

"Maybe?"

"All I know is that one of the characters dies. I haven't entirely decided how, yet," Katya said. "I've been leaning towards a car accident but it might be something different. Like maybe she falls down a staircase."

He straightened up and narrowed his eyes at her. "Your friend died in a car accident."

"So I'm told."

"I was there," he said. "At the scene of the accident. I was the first officer on the scene."

"I see," she said. "It must be a difficult job. Dealing with things like that."

"I'm just proud to serve my community," he said.

"Of course," said Katya.

He put his hands on his hips and said, "Dr. Kaylock was very upset with your visit today. You have to understand she can't give out information about her patients. Even if they're no longer with us."

"I understand," said Katya. "Please do apologize to the doctor for me. I promise it won't happen again."

"See that it doesn't," he said. He leaned in close and lowered his voice. "Your friend, whose other friends have never heard of you, by the way, died in a car accident. End of story. Do you understand?"

She nodded.

"And if I hear about you being anywhere near the coroner's office without being on the table, you'll find yourself arrested for harassment, obstruction, and anything else I can think of. Do I make myself clear?"

She nodded.

"Say, 'Yes, Sheriff'."

"Yes, Sheriff."

"Very well. I'm glad we have an understanding," he said, straightening up again. In his regular voice, he said, "Thank you, ma'am. The Sheriff's department appreciates your understanding and cooperation in this matter."

He departed and Katya closed the door and sat down, shaking. Rose returned from the top of the basement stairs and sat beside her. Vijay, on tiptoe, watched through the door's tiny window until Sheriff Wagner drove away.

"You okay?" he asked Katya.

"Yeah," she said, nodding. "But that was weird, right?"

"He definitely knows more than he's letting on," Vijay said.

"So it's not just me," said Katya.

"Definitely not," Vijay.

They sat in silence for a few moments and then Rose spoke, quietly. "That's his dad," she said.

"I'm sorry?" said Rose.

"That was Bradley's dad. I recognized the voice. He

was there when I fell," she said, not looking at them.

The three sat again in silence for a few more moments, until Vijay said, "So why would he lie about it?"

"You said it was an ornate staircase," said Katya. "I doubt a florist makes enough money to own a fancy home."

"No," Rose said, shaking her head. "It happened at his place. I'm sure of it."

"Maybe he was worried about a lawsuit," Vijay said. "Since it happened on his property."

"Maybe?" said Katya.

Rose stood and said, "Katya, can you take a look at something?"

"Sure, what?"

"My back," she said, unbuttoning her shirt.

Katya stood, gently pulled down the back of Rose's shirt, and said, "There's a bruise. Like, one big splotch between your shoulder blades."

"From a punch," said Rose.

"I mean, maybe?" said Katya. "It's the right size, I guess. And right in the middle of your back."

"Bradley punched me and knocked me down the stairs."

"He punched you in the back?" said Vijay. "So you were walking away from him at the time."

"And his cop dad covered it up," said Katya.

Rose, buttoning her shirt, sat back down.

"And the coroner is in on it," Katya said, sitting down with her.

"Why would he do that?" Vijay asked.

"He was angry with me about something, obviously," said Rose. "But I don't remember what. He was always angry with me about one thing or another."

"No, I meant the coroner," said Vijay. "Why would he

cover something like that up?"

"She," said Katya.

"She? That's even worse," said Vijay. "To the extent that it could be worse."

"It's not a big city," said Katya. "The sheriff could make her life hell pretty easily, I should think."

"He's probably got something on her," Rose said. "I suspect he's got dirt on a lot of people."

"Like what?" Katya asked.

"Who knows?" said Rose, shrugging. "It might not even be real. He could have manufactured something."

"So what do we do?" said Vijay.

"We find Bradley," said Rose.

Twelve

After a search for Bradley and his parents' home address brought up nothing, Katya drove the three of them to Port Hackett and they cruised around what passed for a downtown, looking for anything that might spark a memory.

"Does any of this look familiar?" she asked.

"Kind of?" said Rose. "I mean, we were here this morning. There are a few things that I'm sure I've seen before but nothing specific."

"What if we tried further out?" Vijay said from the back seat. "Maybe check out the residential areas."

"Can't hurt," said Rose.

Katya took them out through highly wooded, old suburban streets to the edge of the town. Further away from the lake were the newer subdivisions. McMansions with large, green lawns. Closer to the lake was a town-wide semicircle of small, cottage-like structures, built not too close to each other, nestled among old, lush forest. Between the cottages and the downtown were the real mansions. Large, old homes belonging to families whose money had been made over a century previously out in the oil fields or the gold rush or via other, less savoury means. It was here that Rose finally said, "Stop!"

Katya hit the brakes.

"Back up. Take that last left."

Katya did as Rose asked. They wound their way among the giant old houses until Rose asked Katya to stop again. To their right, up a long, crescent-shaped driveway was a large stone house. The lights were off but a new sports car sat at the wait outside.

Rose disappeared, leaving only wind in her wake. Katya and Vijay waited in silence for a moment, unsure what to do. The front door of the house opened and Rose motioned to them to come in.

Katya and Vijay looked at each other, each hoping the other would take the lead.

"Is this a good idea?" he asked.

"Probably not."

"Okay, then," Vijay said. "Glad that's sorted," and he opened the door.

They hurried up the driveway and into the darkened, silent house. They stood in a large front hallway decorated in dark browns and off-white. A medieval suit of armour stood on a short riser against the wall to the right. On the left was a painting of a cow in a pasture, held in an ornate frame. Both looked suitably old. Neither Katya nor Vijay knew enough about art to be able to determine if they were in any way valuable, but they certainly looked the part. An ornate chandelier hung above them. Ahead of them, the entryway opened into a wide hallway. In the darkness, they could barely make out a doorway on the far side of the room, and another leading off to the left. To the right, a wide, lush stairway stretched up and around in a half spiral to the upstairs. The wall along the stairway was dotted with more old and expensive-looking paintings.

"This is it. That's the stairway I fell down. And this," she whispered, pointing to the spot under her feet, "is where I died."

Vijay took a step back, partly out of respect but mostly due to being creeped out.

She motioned for them to follow her, and tiptoed quickly up the stairs.

"And this," she whispered, when they reached the top, "is where I was pushed."

Behind her, a hallway stretched out into the darkness. Doors were set into the wall at even intervals.

At the end of the hall, a door opened and a light poured out of it, silhouetting a figure exiting a room.

"Hello?" it said.

Rose grabbed Katya and Vijay by the arm and disappeared, entirely failing to take them with her.

They looked at each other, then looked down the hall at the backlit figure.

"Who's there?" it said.

Rose appeared again and whispered, "I forgot I can't do that. Run!"

They ran.

"Hey!" the figure shouted, and ran after them, but his way was blocked by Rose suddenly appearing directly in front of him, her neck twisted to the side, her head dangling. She opened her mouth and out came a ghastly screech.

The figure screamed, tried to run backwards, and fell over his own feet. Rose disappeared as he hit the floor.

Vijay and Katya jumped into the car and Rose was already in the front seat, laughing hysterically. Katya floored the accelerator and they were off.

"You should have seen the look on his face!" she said.

"Was that him?" said Vijay. "Was that Bradley?"

"Yeah, that was him," said Rose.

"He's not going to sleep right for months," said Vijay.

"Wait, slow down," Rose said. "Turn back around."

"What? Why?"

"There's no way he'll stay home after that. He'll go out drinking with his idiot friends," said Rose. "We should follow him."

Katya thought about it, slowed down, and pulled over. She was still panting. "Are you serious?"

"Absolutely," Rose said, nodding. "I need some answers and I'm sure he has them."

"That's not a terrible idea," said Vijay.

Katya agreed and turned the car around. They stopped at the side of the road just in sight of Bradley's driveway and turned off the car.

They waited in silence for a few minutes before Vijay said, "How does a county sheriff have a house like that?"

"His wife inherited it," said Rose. "She comes from money. He married up."

"And I'm guessing he wants to stay there," said Katya.

They heard a car start up and saw headlights come on. Bradley pulled out of the driveway and took off with no regard for the speed limit.

Katya started the car and took off after him. They reached the first intersection just in time to see him go skidding around the next one to the right. By the time they got there, it was too late. He was nowhere in sight.

"We've lost him," said Katya.

"It's okay," Rose said. "Keep going. I'll tell you when to turn."

"Okay. Where are we going?"

"No idea," said Rose. "I'll know it when we get there."

Katya drove for a few more minutes, following Rose's directions, until they came upon a small, squat building painted to look like a log cabin. Neon advertisements for various liquors and beers littered the windows and strings of triangular banners crisscrossed the patio. The sign out front read "Jimbo's." Bradley's car was there, taking up two parking spaces.

"I know this place," Rose said. "I didn't a couple of minutes ago but I've definitely been here."

Katya parked in the farthest corner of the lot and said, "So what do we do now? You're not thinking of going in there, I hope."

"I don't know," she said. "I need to talk to him."

"In public? That seems like a bad idea," Katya said.

"In private seems like a bad idea too, though," Vijay said.

"So what do we do?" said Rose.

"I have an idea," said Vijay. "I'm assuming his parents paid for some kind of degree?"

"Law," said Rose. "Columbia. He didn't graduate, though."

"Was he in a frat?"

"Alpha Pi Kappa," Rose said.

"Great. You stay here," he said to Rose. "My fiancée Taffy and I are going to go get a drink."

"Taffy?" said Katya.

"Kristal?" he said. "With a K?"

"Can I dot the I with a little heart?"

"Oh, I insist," he said.

"Okay, let's do this," said Katya, and she opened the car door.

The inside of Jimbo's was small, dark, and grimy. It reeked of stale beer and old sweat with an overlay of fried everything. The few patrons who were out on a Tuesday night were mostly on the patio. The only people inside were the bartender and Bradley. Bradley sat in a booth, madly poking at his phone. They sat down at the bar and ordered beers.

"So what now?" Katya asked.

"Hang on," Vijay said. He took a couple of deep breaths and then got up and walked over to Bradley's booth. Katya stayed a few feet behind.

"Bradley?" Vijay said. "Bradley Wagner?"

"Uhhh," Bradley said, looking up from his phone.

"Oh my God! Dude! It *is* you," said Vijay. "It's me, Vivek. From Columbia. Man, I haven't seen you in... How many years now?"

"Oh, uh..." Bradley said.

"Honey, come here, you've gotta meet this guy," Vijay said, beckoning Katya over. "This is Brad. I went to Columbia with him. He was an Alpha Pi Kappa. Those guys had the best parties. Brad, this is my fiancée, Kristal."

"Hi," said Katya.

"Oh my God," Vijay said, sitting down on the other side of the booth. Katya sat beside Bradley. "How've you been, man? What are you doing in Port... Where are we?"

"Hacker," said Katya.

"Yeah, Port Hacker," Vijay said. "What are the chances of running into you here?"

"Hackett," he said, setting his phone on the table, screen-side-down. "I live here."

"No way," Vijay said. "We're just on a little vacation. Driving to Portland to see her family and give them the good news. Right, honey?"

Her hand under the table, Katya surreptitiously pocketed her wedding ring and, beaming, presented her engagement-ring-adorned hand to Bradley. "That's right."

"Uh... great," Bradley said. "Congratulations."

"Thanks," said Katya. "So you knew Vivek back in his wild days, huh? I'll bet you've got all kinds of dirt on him."

"Dirt? On Vivek? Nah. He was a good guy. Never misbehaved," said Bradley, sticking to the Bro Code despite having no idea what was going on.

"Not like Kyle, am I right?" said Vijay, sitting across from Bradley.

"Oh, man, Kyle," he said. "I haven't heard anything from that guy in years."

"Remember when he got wasted at that party at... was it Omega Pi?"

"Omega Psi Phi," Bradley said. "Kind of. I don't remember much of their parties."

"I hear that," Vijay said, giving Bradley's bottle a cheers. "So how about you? What are you doing with yourself these days?"

"I got a job at a law firm here in town," he said.

"Oh, so you're practicing?"

"Well, no," he said. "I'm still a couple of credits short so I can't actually practice, but I can do other stuff. I'll go back eventually. Maybe. This job's pretty good. Low stress."

"That's great," Vijay said. "What's the place called?"

"Wagner and Browne."

"Wagner?" Vijay said. "Any relation?"

"Yeah, it's, uh... it's my mom's firm," he said, looking at the table.

"Oh, well, hey, that's cool," Vijay said. "Keeping it in the family, right? Maybe you can take it over one day."

"Yeah, that's the plan."

"Speaking of family, you got any of your own? Wife?

Kids?"

"Uh, no," he said. "Not yet."

"Not ready to settle down yet, eh?"

"Something like that."

"You still got that girlfriend? What was her name? That super cute one."

"Meri?" he said. "The Australian one?"

"No, no, that other one. The brunette," said Vijay.

"Jennifer?"

"No, what was her name? Her mom owned a flower shop," Vijay said. Then he snapped his fingers and said, "Rose!"

Bradley snapped backward and his eyes went wide. "What? Who are you? What do you want from me?"

"What do you mean?"

Bradley half-stood, put his fists on the table, knuckles-down, and leaned forward. "Who the hell are you?"

"It's me, Vivek," said Vijay. "Are you telling me you don't remember me?"

"No, I don't remember you because I've never seen you before in my life," said Bradley, sticking a finger in Vijay's face. "I don't know what you want but you need to leave. Immediately."

While he was speaking, the door opened and two more men came in. One was short and wore a crisp, grey suit. The other was over six feet tall and ripped. He wore an armless t-shirt that read *Bro, I Don't Even Lift* in an attempt at ironic humour.

"Bro, what's up?" said the short guy. "Who's this?"

"He claims his name's Vivek," said Bradley. "Says he went to Columbia with us."

"I never seen him before," said the short one. "Kai?"

"Nah, I ain't never seen him in my life," said the big one.

"Come on, guys. It's me. Vivek," said Vijay. "You remember me. I was Kevin's roommate."

"Steve was Kevin's roommate," said the big guy. "Ain't that right, Blaine?"

"Yeah, that's right."

"Not that Kevin," said Vijay. "The other Kevin. Kevin Reuckert."

"Never heard of him," said Bradley.

"I think it's time for you to leave," said Blaine. "Right, Kai?"

"Right."

"Yeah, okay. Sure," said Vijay, getting up. Kai put his hand on Vijay's shoulder and pushed him back down again.

Blaine leaned down to Vijay's ear and said, "If we see you again, you won't be going anywhere, you understand? We've dealt with bigger than you before and they all ended up sorry. You got it?"

Vijay gulped and nodded.

"And don't think bringing your soulless ginger bitch with you is going to help anything because we're equal opportunity here. What happens to you happens to her. Am I making myself clear?"

"Uh, yeah," said Vijay, continuing to nod.

"Great. Get the hell out of here."

They hurried back to the car and sat, shaking. Katya rested her head on the steering wheel and rubbed her chest wound.

"Are you okay?" Vijay asked her.

"Yeah," she said. "Did you see his face when you mentioned Rose?"

"That was not a normal grief reaction."

"No, it was not," she said.

"What the hell happened?" Rose asked. And they told her the story.

"Man, I wish I could hear what they're discussing right now," said Rose.

"We can," Vijay said. "As soon as I get my phone back."

"Wait, what?" said Katya. "Where is your phone?"

"In Blaine's jacket pocket."

"What is it doing there?"

"Recording."

"But... but how will you get it back?"

"That depends," said Vijay. He turned to Rose. "Have you ever been to Blaine's place?"

"Yeah, I think so."

Three hours later, with Katya's phone tracking Vijay's, they were parked outside of Blaine's condo.

"Are you sure you're okay to do this?" Katya said. But she hadn't completed the sentence when Rose disappeared. She reappeared a moment later and held out her empty hand to Vijay.

"Shit," she said and disappeared again.

The front door of Blaine's condo opened a few minutes later and Rose came running back to the car. She jumped in and Katya drove away as Rose handed Vijay his phone.

"Good stuff," he said.

"Is it okay?" she asked. "I kind of dropped it when I did that first return blink."

"Yeah, it's fine. Battery's a little low and my storage is maxed but that's to be expected."

"Okay, good," Rose said.

"I don't understand why you can't move things when you blink," said Katya.

"That's the thing that's most confusing to you about all of this?" Rose said.

"Well, no. But..."

"But your clothes go with you," Vijay said.

"Apparently," said Rose.

"What would happen if you put something in your pockets?" Vijay asked.

"They're women's clothes," said Katya. "They don't have any pockets."

Rose chuckled and said, "I actually do have two little pockets in here. You got any coins or anything?"

Vijay handed Rose a quarter. She put it in her pocket and disappeared. The coin fell to the seat of the car. Rose reappeared and said, "No luck."

"That is really weird," Vijay said.

They arrived home as the sun was rising. All three were exhausted but fired up at the same time. Vijay dusted off an old boombox and found an adapter cable so they could listen to the recording on better speakers than the one on his phone. It was still unclear. The voices were muffled from being in Blaine's pocket and the background noise nearly blotted them out entirely but they heard scraps.

"I thought we agreed we'd never talk about it."

...

"It couldn't possibly have been her."

...

"You saw her neck. Nobody could live through that."
"Huh huh. That was brutal."

...

"Could it be Kaylock screwing with us?"
"She wouldn't dare. Your dad basically owns her."

...

"I'm telling you it was her! It was Rose!"
"You need to calm down..."
"Don't tell me to calm down!"

...

"You idiots are of no help!"
"Hey, I'm not the one that did it."

"Not so loud!"

They eventually went their separate ways and Katya stopped the playback.

"We should take this to the cops," said Vijay. They stared at him, incredulously. "Not the local cops, obviously."

"Even then, I feel like that's a good way to end up dead," said Katya. "No offense."

"None taken," said Rose. "I think you're probably right. Besides, it's hardly conclusive."

"So what do we do?" Vijay said.

"We sleep on it," said Rose. "Or, rather, you sleep on it and I sit around and read or something. And we reconvene this evening after work."

"That's probably a good idea," said Katya, looking at the time. "I have to be at work in like four hours."

"Maybe you should call in again," said Vijay.

"No," said Rose. "You two need to act like nothing is weird. You're already on the sheriff's radar. If Bradley mentions anything about this to him, he's going to put two and two together."

"I think she's right," said Vijay.

Katya, nodding, said, "Yeah. Let's get some sleep. Those of us who do."

Thirteen

Katya and Vijay returned home early the next evening to find a house that had been straightened, vacuumed, and dusted. The dishes were done and dinner was being made.

"You didn't have to do this," said Katya.

"I wanted to. You've been so good to me," said Rose. "I mean, except for the whole hitting-me-with-an-umbrella thing. But that was understandable, considering the circumstances."

They had dinner and the three of them curled up on the sofa and watched some mindless TV for a while. Eventually, Vijay said, "So did anybody think of a plan?"

"I've got nothing," said Katya. "You?"

"Nope," Vijay said, shaking his head. "Rose?"

"I have a couple of thoughts."

"Oh?" said Vijay.

"Can I borrow your phone?"

"Sure," he said, and handed it over.

"It's star-six-seven to hide Caller ID, right?"

"Uh, yeah," said Vijay. "But I'm not sure I like where this is going."

"Oh, I do," Katya said, sitting up straight.

Rose punched a few digits into the phone and waited. Vijay and Katya, sitting perfectly silent, holding their breath, heard Bradley answer.

"Hello?" he said, groggily.

In a small, breathy voice, Rose said, "Why did you leave me buried out there?"

She disconnected and laughed outrageously. Katya soon joined in. Vijay sat with his mouth agape for a moment while Rose returned his phone to him, but it didn't take long before he broke.

"Okay, that was pretty good," he said. "I wish I could have seen the look on his face."

"Why do I have a feeling that's only the beginning?" said Katya.

"Because I'm going to make that bastard wish he could trade places with me."

Fourteen

It was shortly after three a.m. Most of the denizens of Port Hackett were asleep. But not Rose.

Rose stood in front of the Wagner house. All of the lights were out. So were the mosquitoes, but they paid her no mind. She walked along the side of the road, past a heavily wooded area, until she came to the Wagners' closest neighbour. Their house was as old and grandiose as the Wagners'. But it didn't have what she needed. The opposite side of the street had no houses at all. It was still old-growth forest. A city by-law protected that land, preventing any new structures from being built on it. Penelope Wagner was highly involved in making that by-law pass. For the good of the environment and the integrity of the town, of course. The fact that it helped to protect her property values had nothing to do with it.

Rose continued walking until she found the house she was looking for. Surrounded by an iron gate and set far back from the street, the giant wall-sized trellis could just be made out in the dark.

With a gust of wind, she appeared at the side of the house. She picked a rose from the wall and headed back to the street.

She reached through the gate and set the flower on the ground. Then she appeared on the outside of the gate, picked up the rose, and walked back the way she had come.

Quietly, she snuck into the Wagners' yard and around back. In the rear of the house was a set of large, modern, sliding glass doors that led out to a multi-level deck with a barbecue larger than most people's stoves. Sam Wagner didn't cook but he liked to apply fire to meat a couple of weekends every summer when he had the boys over to watch the game.

To one side of the deck was a disused, nearly-forgotten door that led to what had been a pantry in the old days, before refrigeration. Now it was mostly used to store old board games that hadn't been played in well over a decade.

Rose approached the pantry door quietly but she triggered the motion detector and the outdoor lights came on.

She didn't worry too much about that. The security lights went largely ignored since the trigger was almost always a raccoon or a squirrel. Still, her white dress didn't blend in with the scenery so she threw the rose towards the door and then blinked inside.

She stood just inside the pantry door and listened. There was no noise inside the house. Through the little window beside the door, she saw the light go out. She unlocked the door, opened it, and reached out slowly to grab the rose.

Then she locked the door again and crept through the house.

At the top of the stairs, she stopped and listened.

Nothing. She continued on to the main floor.

As she approached the main staircase in the front hall, she heard footsteps. Someone was coming down the stairs.

She ducked through the doorway on her right, into the kitchen, and to the back of the room.

The figure from the stairway followed her, grunting, and approached the refrigerator. But she was already gone.

Lurking in the hallway, she peeked into the kitchen and saw Sam by the light of the fridge. He took a drink of milk right from the container, burped, and sighed. As he closed the refrigerator door, he muttered, "The hell?" and bent down to pick up the rose.

"Where'd you come from?" he said, and deposited it in the trash. Then he made a quick detour to the washroom before heading back up the stairs.

After hearing his door close, Rose fished the flower out of the trash and followed him.

She tiptoed down the hallway to Bradley's room, where she stopped and listened. She could hear him snoring. Flattening the rose between her palms, she knelt down. She slid the stem under the door, flattened the head some more, and pushed it through, as well. Then she blinked to the other side.

She could hear Bradley sleeping, but his room was too dark to see anything. She retrieved the rose and tiptoed to the side of his bed. There, she reached out, flower in hand, and held it about three feet above his face.

Then she screamed, let go of the rose, and blinked away.

Fifteen

Sam opened his eyes and muttered, "What now?"

Beside him, Penelope stirred. "What was that?"

"I'll check it out," Sam said, and hauled himself out of bed. He stepped into the hall and saw light coming through the crack under Bradley's door.

"Of course," he muttered.

He walked to Bradley's room and banged on the door harder than was necessary. Bradley let out a shocked cry.

"Everything all right in there?" said Sam.

"Uh... I uh..."

"I thought I heard a woman scream," Sam said.

The door whipped open and Bradley looked at Sam, wide-eyed and manic. "I didn't hear anything."

"You got a girl in there?" said Sam.

"What? Me? No," Bradley said, avoiding eye contact.

Sam pushed the door open and walked in. "Why did I hear a woman scream?"

"I, um..."

Sam spotted the rose sitting on the floor, where it

had landed after Bradley had thrown it in a panic.

"The hell is this?"

"I think it's a flower," Bradley said, pacing and running his hand through his hair.

"I can see it's a flower," said Sam. "Why is it here?"

"Uh..."

"I found one just like it in the kitchen a few minutes ago."

"You did? Weird," said Bradley.

"Look, I don't care if you have a girl in here, just keep it down, okay?"

"Uh, yeah," said Bradley. "Okay. Sure."

"Okay, then," said Sam, and he left the room.

He walked towards his room and realized that he was still holding the rose. He sighed and took it downstairs to throw out. When he opened the cupboard with the garbage in it and saw that there was no flower in it, he furrowed his brow.

He hung onto the rose and went back upstairs. The light in Bradley's room was still on. He knocked and said, "Hey. I'm coming in."

He gave Bradley a second to hide the girl in his room, but didn't hear any rustling. He opened the door to find Bradley sitting on the edge of the bed, shaking, his head in his hands.

"You wanna tell me what's going on?"

"Nothing."

"Oh really? Someone woke me up screaming last night, and then just now I heard a girl scream, then heard you scream, then I find you acting all weird and twitchy," said Sam. "And you've got this flower in your room that I found on the kitchen floor and threw out barely ten minutes ago. You need to tell me what the hell is going on."

"I don't know," said Bradley. "Nothing. It's fine."

"I've been a cop longer than you've been alive," Sam said. "I know when people are lying. And you're real bad at it. Fess up."

Bradley squirmed and looked around the room at nothing. "You're gonna think I'm crazy."

"I already think you're an idiot, so crazy might be an upgrade," said Sam. "Talk."

"You'll never believe me."

"Try me."

"Dad?"

"What?"

"It's her," said Bradley.

"Her who?"

Bradley nodded at the rose in Sam's hand and said, "Her. Rose."

After a pause, he said, "Rose who?"

"You know exactly who, Dad. Rose. Rose Kaidan."

"Rose Kaidan is dead, dumbass."

"I know she is," said Bradley. "I was there, remember?"

"Oh, I remember," Sam said. "I remember cleaning up your goddamned mess, as usual. Now why don't you tell me what the hell is going on?"

"It was her. Last night," he said. He looked up at his dad for the first time since he'd entered the room. "The scream."

"Elaborate."

"I thought I heard a noise so I got up and she was in the hallway. She screamed at me and disappeared."

"She couldn't have been in the hallway," Sam said. "She's dead."

"I know! She was dead and her neck was broken but she was in the hallway."

"You imagined it," said Sam. "You're stressed. You need to chill."

"I didn't imagine it. I know what I saw."

"Then you dreamed it or something. There's no way she was here."

"Then who screamed?"

Sam glared at Bradley, not wanting to admit that he had a good point.

"You heard it," Bradley said. "You heard her scream. Who else could it have been?"

"Not her," Sam said. "But I'm going to get to the bottom of whatever's going on."

Sixteen

The following afternoon, while her friends were at work, Rose was alphabetizing the book shelf when she heard a key in the lock.

"You're home early," she called.

"Uh, hello?" said a voice that belonged to neither Katya nor Vijay.

Rose dropped the copy of Kari Maaren's *Weave A Circle Round* she was filing and blinked into the living room to grab her sunglasses from the coffee table. She put them on just as the mystery person entered the room, carrying a backpack.

"Uh... hello," said Amar.

"Oh. You must be Vijay's brother."

"Oh, you just assume I'm Vijay's brother? Why, because I'm brown? So I must be related to Vijay?"

"Um..."

"Nah, I'm just messing with you. Of course I'm Vijay's brother," he said, offering his hand and smiling. "I'm Amar."

"Rose," she said, shaking his hand. "I'm an old

friend of Katya's."

"Hi, Rose. Wow, you're really cold," he said. "Vij won't let you touch the thermostat?"

She chuckled and said, "No, I've just got some circulation issues."

"Oh, nothing serious, I hope."

"No, I'm fine. Thanks."

"Cool, cool," he said. "Cool shades. Inside. I can dig it."

"Yeah, my pupils are permanently dilated," she said. "Like Bowie."

"Oh, I love Bowie," Amar said. "He's a big inspiration to guys like me."

"Indian guys?"

"Nope." He stood there awkwardly for a moment. "I was just dropping this off for Vijay," he said, proffering the backpack. "Is that cool?"

"Sure."

"Thanks," he said, "I'll just put it away for him."

"Sure," said Rose.

Amar took the bag to the basement. In a small room at the back of the house that was originally used for coal storage, he pried a sheet of wood paneling aside and hid the bag.

"Thanks again," he said on the way out. And he noticed the Big Board. "Whoa, what's all this?"

"Oh, uh... Katya's decided to write a novel."

"Seriously? That's awe... some..."

He trailed off as he took in the notes on the three-by-five cards; *Zombie? No Eyes. Cold.*

His eyes darted to Rose, back to the board, and back to Rose again.

"Right, well... I should go. It was good to meet you," Amar said, and got out as quickly as was polite.

Seventeen

It was three thirty-two a.m. and Rose stood in the living room being fussed over by Katya and Vijay.

"Are you sure that's going to be warm enough?" said Katya, referring to her funeral dress.

"I won't be out long. Besides, am I going to catch a cold?"

"I don't know, can you?"

"Honestly, I have no idea," Rose said. "I don't think so."

"What about food?" Katya said. "I've got protein bars."

"I can't take anything with me, though," said Rose.

"Vijay can drive you," said Katya. "Can't you, Vijay?"

"Sure, if you want."

"It's fine," Rose said. "I can be there and back before you could drive to the end of the block."

"What about a rain coat? It's coming down pretty hard out there. You can wear that, right?"

"That'll ruin my carefully-cultivated look," Rose said. "Speaking of, how's my mud?"

Katya regarded the mud from the backyard that Rose had smeared down the side of her face. "Like you just crawled out of the grave."

"Aww, thanks."

"Okay," said Katya. "You be careful. We're here for you if you need us."

"I know. Thanks," Rose said, and she disappeared.

Rose appeared in the side yard of Bradley's parents' house. The sudden change from indoors to cold wind and rain was startling. Lightning flashed, briefly revealing the house in stark contrast. She took a moment to get her bearings and figured out which window was Bradley's. It was the second window from the back on the second floor.

She walked closer to the back of the house, paused, looked at the window, and blinked. She reappeared, standing on the window ledge, knocked three times, slowly, and blinked back to the lawn.

She waited a few moments and did it again, this time knocking harder.

The drapes moved aside and Bradley looked out just as a flicker of lightning illuminated the yard. His jaw dropped when he saw her. In the darkness between lightning, she blinked closer to the house and waited for the next bolt. It came just a moment later. She could hear Bradley's scream through the walls.

That was enough for now. She blinked back home, where Katya was waiting with a towel.

She laughed uproariously as she told the story to Katya and Vijay.

Eighteen

Vijay and Amar sat in a remote corner of a coffee shop on the outskirts of downtown Port Langston.

"So do you care to tell me what you were doing with a computer?"

"Well, I'm a computer nerd," said Amar. "Have been for a long time. Remember when you taught me to write a 'HELLO_WORLD'?"

"Did you forget that you're on probation and you're not allowed to own a computer?"

"Of course not," said Amar. "That's why I took it over to your place."

"Where'd you get it?"

"Doesn't matter," Amar said. "Who's the young lady you've got living with you?"

"It matters," said Vijay. "Her name is Rose. She's an old friend of Katya's."

"Katya's never mentioned her before."

"There's probably lots of things you don't know about her," said Vijay. "Have you been hanging out with your hacker friends?"

"She seems kind of young to be an old friend. And define 'hanging out'."

"Spending time with in a manner that a reasonable jury might consider 'associating'," Vijay said. "And Katya used to babysit her."

"Well, if that's the definition you're going with, then I suppose I have," Amar said. "And that's not the same as being an old friend."

"Semantics."

"In both cases."

"Look, dude," Vijay said. "You can't get caught. You can't go back to jail again."

"I won't."

"Is it stolen?"

"No, it was mine before I got arrested. I left it with a frie—an associate," he corrected, "for safekeeping. Is she a zombie?"

"But, again, you aren't allowed to own or use a computer," said Vijay. "And what are you talking about?"

"That's why I took it to your place," Amar said. "Rose. Is she a zombie?"

"There are no such things as zombies. And what happens if I'm found with it?"

"Well, if the accepted mythology is anything to go by, it eats your brains."

"The laptop," said Vijay. "What happens if I'm found with the laptop?"

"Nothing. You're allowed to own as many computers as you want," said Amar. "So is she some sort of ghoul?"

"Don't be ridiculous," said Vijay. "What about the software?"

"Oh, the software? Yeah, you don't want to get caught with that software," Amar said. "But you won't because they'd have no reason to search your house and they'd have no reason to be given a warrant. And even if they did, you could deny all knowledge, throw me under the bus, and you'd be fine."

"You know I wouldn't."

"I'd be fine with it if you did," said Amar. "You've got a wife to take into account. And possibly a way-younger girlfriend."

Vijay sighed and said, "She is in no way my girlfriend."

Amar opened his mouth to speak but Vijay cut him off. "No, she's not Kat's girlfriend, either."

"So what is she?"

"I told you, Katya used to be her tutor," said Vijay.

"You said 'babysitter'."

"Did I?"

"Yeah."

"A person can be two things," Vijay said.

"We're both terrible liars, aren't we?" said Amar.

"We get it from Dad."

"Yeah," Amar said. "So what is she?"

"Honestly, you wouldn't believe me if I told you."

"Try me."

Vijay sighed and sat back in his chair. "Well, I got home from my trip the other night and she and Kat were in the living room..."

Nineteen

Three thirty-four a.m. The waxing gibbous moon glowed faintly through the space between the window and the drapes, illuminating a blurry stripe across Bradley's face. Rose, once again wearing her funeral dress, her face smeared with mud, stood at the foot of his bed.

She remembered, vaguely, seeing him in the flower shop for the first time. He said he was buying flowers for his mom and asked for Rose's number. She was reluctant but her mom encouraged her. "He seems a nice boy," she had said. "How many boys buy flowers for their moms?"

Strange, then, that when she met his mother for the first time, and his mother had learned that Rose worked in a flower shop, she commented that nobody had bought her flowers in a long time.

She went on to interrogate Rose on her future plans, commenting that nobody who is worth anything should work in a flower shop their whole lives. Even if they own it. *Especially* if they own it. A real business owner should want more, she said. Business itself should be what they love. The specific business shouldn't matter. Just as long as it's profitable.

Rose stood gazing at Bradley's sleeping face, listening to him snore, waiting for him to stir. But he was in too deep a sleep and Rose grew impatient. She gave the footboard a little kick. Not too hard, as her feet were bare.

Nothing. She kicked again, then reached down and gave the blankets a little tug. He stirred a bit, stopped snoring, and rolled onto his back. But he went back to sawing logs.

She pulled the blanket up to reveal his feet, one of which she touched with her cold hand.

He stirred, opened his eyes, saw Rose, frowned, and, still groggy, closed his eyes again. A moment later his eyes shot open and he scrambled to a sitting position, and turned on the light. But Rose had already disappeared, leaving nothing but a small wind in her wake.

Twenty

"Bradley? Bradley!" shouted his mother, Penelope Simons-Wagner. She had kept the Simons surname after marriage, not as any sort of feminist statement, but because the Simons family name still carried weight in Langston County. Being married to the sheriff had its advantages, but not to the extent that she could give up the benefits of being a member of one of the most influential families in the area.

"Hmm? What?" he said, pulling his distracted gaze away from the office window.

"Do you have the numbers?"

"Oh, yeah. Yes," he said, handing over a folder.

"Not to me, to the client," she said, and Bradley slid the folder across the meeting room table to an old man in a suit. Bradley had been told his name a few minutes earlier but had already forgotten.

"I think these are, um..." he stammered. "These are... the... uh... numbers."

"I think what my son is trying to say," said Penelope, "is that these figures should be to your liking, Mr.

Howland."

Mr. Howland took a look at the papers and said, "These look agreeable, certainly. Of course, I'll have my people look over them before I sign anything."

"Of course, Mr. Howland," she said. "I'm sure your people will find everything in order. If you have any questions or concerns, please feel free to give us a call at any time."

"Very well. Thank you, Mrs. Wagner."

After he took his leave, Penelope's smile dropped and she spun around to face Bradley. "What the hell is wrong with you?"

"I, uh..."

"You're more out of it than usual. Your hair is unkempt. Your shirt is partially untucked. And don't even get me started on that tie. I know it's Sunday but you've known for over a week that you'd need to come in today."

There was a knock at the door and Blaine waltzed in. "Hey, boss. I just saw the elder Howland walking out of here. How'd it go?"

"It went well, Blaine, thank you for asking," she said. "No thanks to your friend, here. You need to stop having him out late drinking and whoring every night. Apparently he doesn't have your stamina."

"Really? We were in early last night. Maybe he's turning into a lightweight in his old age," he said, giving Bradley a light punch on the shoulder. Bradley just stared, bleary-eyed, out the window.

"Well, whatever it is, it stops now," said Penelope. "I'm making him your responsibility."

"Understood, ma'am," he said. "You can count on me."

"Prove it with actions, Mr. Carstairs," she said, and left the room.

As soon as the door closed, Blaine spun on Bradley and said, "Dude, what's wrong with you? You look like shit. I mean, more so than usual."

"It was her again," he said, continuing to stare at nothing. "Last night."

"Jesus, not this again."

"She was in my room."

"Right, of course. In your room," Blaine said. "First she screamed at you, then she showed up for some flower delivery, then she was on your lawn. And now in your room."

"It's her. I know it's her. She's come back for me."

"To do what? Scream and stand there?"

"To kill me? Torture me? Drag me to Hell?" said Bradley. "I don't know. But it's her and she's back."

"She can't be back," Blaine said. "She's dead. You killed her. You're just feeling guilty or something. But you can't. You need to get it together. Understand? You got away with it. Now let it go."

"Will you stay with me tonight?"

"Hell, no, I won't stay with you tonight. Or any night," Blaine said. "You're a grown man. Give your balls a tug and act like one."

Bradley continued to stare out the window.

"Come on," said Blaine. "Let's knock off early. Get a couple of beers. And maybe some scotch. I know where we can get a fantastic thirty-year-old single malt. Waddya say?"

Bradley turned his head and made eye contact with Blaine. He blinked and came back to the real world. "Scotch, yeah. Scotch sounds good."

"Of course you wake up when I mention the expensive stuff," said Blaine. "Let's go. You're buying."

Twenty-One

That night, after a long talk with Blaine and Kai, in which they tried, mostly successfully, to convince him that he had imagined everything, and after sufficiently medicating himself with copious amounts of alcohol, Bradley crawled into bed.

In the dead of night, he was awakened by a thumping sound.

He opened his eyes and tried to concentrate through an alcoholic fog. There it was again; a loud thump from across the room. He reached out for his bedside lamp and switched it on, but nothing happened. The thump happened again, twice.

Bradley sat up and tried to clear his head. He was still buzzed but the hangover was starting to move in. Tomorrow's headache was going to be a nasty one.

The thump happened again. Three times, slowly.

He heard another thumping, this one deep in his ears, as his heart rate increased. The sound of it blocked out everything else. Except for the thumping coming from across the room. His closet door shook with each noise.

The closet was between the bed and the door. In order to leave the room, he'd have to walk past it. He got out of bed and approached the closet, which continued to thud and shake. He crouched down a few feet away from it and stretched out his hand, trying to keep as far away from the closet as possible. His fingertips closed around the handle and the knocking stopped. He turned the handle slowly. The door opened with a creak to reveal nothing but clothes.

Bradley straightened up and approached the closet. Cautiously, he poked around inside it, moved a few shirts to the side and peered in, looking for anywhere a person could hide. There was nowhere. Nobody was in his closet. He shut the door, closed his eyes, leaned his forehead against the closet and exhaled in relief. After a few more deep breaths, he opened his eyes and turned around to go back to bed.

The filthy, eyeless spectre of his murdered girlfriend screamed in his face.

Bradley joined in with a scream of his own and pitched backwards into the closet door. She lunged towards him. He closed his eyes, turned to one side with his leg up for protection, and covered his face with his arms.

Instead of the excruciating pain he expected, he felt only a wind and heard her scream suddenly cut off while his own continued.

He stood on one leg, the rest of his body squeezed up against the closet door, shaking. He opened one eye and looked around. She was gone. He gradually put his leg down and lowered his arms. His breathing and heart rate lowered.

He turned around and opened the closet door again, just to be sure. Leaving it open, he walked, on shaking legs, back to the bed and sat down on the edge, looking around the room and trying to process what had just happened.

He felt the mattress move and caught movement out of the corner of his eye. His blanket rose up at the head of the bed and then fell, revealing Rose, her head hanging at the side of her body.

"Why did you kill me?" she said in her gravelly voice.

Bradley screamed and ran out of the room. She appeared in the hallway in front of him, and he turned and ran back towards his room. She blinked into his room and slammed the door shut. He crashed into it. He stumbled backwards and landed on his ass. She blinked through the door and approached him. He crab-walked away from her in a panic, landed on his elbows, and spun around onto his front and scrabbled back upright. He ran towards the stairway again. When he reached the top of it, she appeared behind him and pushed. He went tumbling down as his dad came out of his own room, shouting, "What the hell is going on out here?"

Sam's eyes widened when he saw Rose. She blinked into the space directly in front of him and screamed. He took a quick step backwards and threw a punch. His fist connected with wind and she reappeared at the top of the stairs in time to see that Bradley had survived the fall. He ran outside, leaving the front door wide open.

Bradley jumped into his car and floored it. Rose appeared in the road in front of him and he aimed right for her but she disappeared at the last second.

Speeding along the back roads, he called Blaine, but he didn't answer. He tried Kai, who picked up.

"Bro, what's up?"

"She was here!" he said. "She was in my room!"

"Who, that skank from the Dynasty?"

"No, Rose! She was in my closet and her neck was broken and she attacked me."

"Whatever, bro," Kai said. "Are you high?"

"No, I'm not high," he said. "Okay, a little, but that's beside the point. It was her. I'm on my way over."

"What? Why?"

"Because we need a plan of attack," he said. "Just meet me outside your place. I'll be there in a couple of minutes and we'll go get Blaine."

"Fine," said Kai, and he hung up.

Twelve minutes later, he came skidding up to Kai's place to find him waiting out front, looking annoyed.

Just as he approached, Rose popped up in the back seat and screeched, "Why did you kill me?"

Bradley screamed, jerked the wheel to the side and accidentally hit the accelerator. He plowed into Kai, who popped up over the hood and into the windshield, cracking it.

Bradley jumped out of the car and fell onto the gravel. He spun around to see Kai roll off of the hood of the car accompanied by a stream of expletives.

"Dude, look out!" said Bradley.

"It's a little late for that."

"No, bro! She's in the car."

Kai groaned and tried to stand. "I think my leg is broken."

"That's the least of your worries, dude."

"It's really not," said Kai.

"Dude, she's in the car and she's going to kill us both."

Wincing, Kai pulled himself up on one knee and looked. "She's not in the car, bro."

"She was just there."

"Well there's nobody in there now."

Bradley's phone rang. It was his dad. "I can't talk

right now."

"You're going to goddamned talk right now," said Sam. "Just what the hell was that all about?"

"You know what it was."

"Don't start that crap again," said Sam.

"It's not crap," said Bradley. "She's back from the dead. And I think she wants to kill me."

"It's obviously your idiot friends screwing with you," Sam said. "Are they with you?"

"Kai's here. I broke his leg."

"Serves him right, the damned idiot."

"No, I lost control of the car when she appeared and I ran into him."

"Put him on the phone," said Sam.

Bradley handed Kai the phone. "Yeah?"

"Are you pulling some kind of bullshit prank on my idiot kid?"

"No, sir."

"You swear?"

"I swear," said Kai. "I think he's losing it. Seeing things."

"I'm not seeing things," said Bradley.

"Well, whatever he's seeing, I saw it, too," Sam said. "And if it turns out to be you and that other idiot, I'm sending you both to see Dr. Kaylock. You understand?"

"I understand," said Kai. "Can you tell Brad to take me to a hospital?"

"No. Walk it off."

"I can't."

"Tough. Where's Blaine?"

"I don't know."

"Put Idiot Number One back on the phone."

Kai tossed the phone back to Bradley and rolled over on his side, still clutching at his leg.

"Dad?"

"Where the hell is that other idiot?"

"Blaine?"

"No, the Pope," said Sam. "Of course, Blaine. How many other idiots do you hang out with?"

"Uh..."

"Yeah, don't bother answering that. Where is he?"

"At home, I guess."

"Go to his place now. I'll meet you there in ten."

"Should I take Kai to the hospital?"

"No," he said, and hung up.

Ten minutes later, Sam rolled up in front of Blaine's condo and hit the buzzer repeatedly. Bradley arrived thirty seconds later. He ran up to the building, his head on a swivel. "She could be anywhere," he said.

Kai eased himself out of the car and limped towards the condo.

"Jesus H, you look like shit, kid," said Sam, still hammering on the buzzer.

The window closest to the entrance slid open and a man stuck his head out. "Hey, asshole! It's four in the morning!"

Sam pointed a gun at the man and said, "This doesn't concern you."

In apparent agreement, the man closed the window.

Finally, Blaine's voice rang out, thin and trebly, through the little speaker. "Unless this is Halle Berry looking to give a blow job, you're about to die."

"Halle Berry wishes she was as hot as me," said Sam. "Get the hell down here."

Static sounded through the system for a moment until Blaine said, "I'll be right down."

Blaine emerged two minutes later, in his suit and tie, his hair perfect. "What's going on?"

Sam gestured with a nod of his head to where the cars were parked, then he walked in that direction. They followed him there, Kai lagging behind. "What the hell happened to you?" Blaine asked.

"Dumbass ran me down with his car because there was a zombie in it."

"Oh, so just an average Saturday, then," said Blaine.

They all climbed into Sam's car. "Away from ears that can't mind their own business," he said. "Now if either of you know anything about what's going on here, you need to come clean right now before Demi Moore here talks too loudly about things he shouldn't be talking about at all. Understand? Good. Now who knows what? Blaine, go."

"He told us she was haunting him so we told him to get it together. Last night I took him out to blow off some steam and then dropped him off a few hours ago."

"Kai?" said Sam.

"Same thing. Then he called me like twenty minutes ago, said he was coming over, and ran into me. He said she was in the car."

"It's her," said Bradley. "She pushed me down the stairs. She's come back for revenge. You saw her."

"You saw her?" Blaine asked Sam.

"I saw something," Sam said. "It wasn't her. It was smoke and mirrors or something."

"It was her," said Bradley. "She can teleport."

"Nobody can teleport," said Sam.

"Ghosts can."

"Ghosts aren't real," Sam said. "Grow up."

"This one is."

"Shut up. Now, we're going to figure out what's going on and stop it," said Sam. "And nobody is going to mention the incident in public. Or anywhere else, for that matter."

"Great," said Blaine. "Where do we start?"

"First stop is the hospital," said Sam, starting the car.

"Oh, thank Christ," said Kai.

"Cut your whining," Sam said. "Blaine, take Kai in your car and meet us there. Brad, you're coming with me."

"What about my car?" said Bradley.

"We'll come back for it later," Sam said. "You're in no shape to drive right now, anyway."

They drove off, not noticing the eyeless face watching them from the back seat of Bradley's car.

Twenty-Two

In the hospital parking lot, Blaine helped Kai out of the car.

"By the way, you fell down the stairs," said Sam.

"Yeah, I had way too much to drink."

"Shocker," said Sam.

Sam used his clout to get Kai taken care of ahead of other patients. He assured the doctors that, despite his skittishness and apparent non-engagement with his surroundings, Bradley was perfectly okay. "He's just been up too long and he's worried about his friend. He'll be fine."

He left Bradley on an uncomfortable plastic chair in a hallway and dragged Blaine around a corner to talk in private.

"Why is it you're the only one of my son's friends I can count on when shit hits the fan around here?"

"Because I know how to hold my liquor and don't spend all of my spare time playing video games?"

"Liquor. Sure, that's what you're holding," said Sam. Blaine gave a noncommittal half-shrug.

"Listen. I don't know what's going on, but it's not nothing," Sam said. "I saw something. Something I can't explain. Yet."

"What kind of something?"

"Something that somebody wanted me to think was you-know-who," said Sam. "Whoever's doing this scared the crap out of my pussy-ass excuse for a son. And I don't know how they did it, but I suspect I know who it was."

"Who?"

"This woman was snooping around Kaylock's office the other day. Katya Carter. You ever heard of her?"

"Doesn't ring a bell."

"Well, she was asking about you-know-who," Sam said. "And she knew things she shouldn't know."

"Maybe we should pay her a visit," said Blaine. As he spoke, they heard Bradley scream. Blaine ran around the corner and collided with him coming the other direction. Bradley, terror in his eyes, tried to push Blaine to the side.

"What the hell, bro?" Blaine said, grabbing Bradley by the arm. "What's wrong?"

"She's here!" Bradley screamed. He spun around and pointed at an empty gurney. He flicked his head around wildly, looking for her. "She was right there! There was a body on the stretcher and it sat up and it was her!"

"Okay, well, she's not there now, right?" Blaine asked. "Do you see her now?"

"No."

"So it's fine. Calm down. She's gone."

"That's worse!" he said. "She could be anywhere!"

"Sir, are you feeling okay?" a passing nurse asked.

"How do you stop a dead person?" Bradley asked her.

"He's fine," Sam said. "He's just had a long day, is all."

"I need to stop her," Bradley said. "She's after me and I need to stop her."

"Are you sure?" the nurse asked. "Because this looks a lot more serious than just a long day."

"I said he's fine! Get back to work."

"How do I kill the dead?"

Glowering, the nurse kept her mouth shut and went looking for someone with more authority.

"Okay, now just you calm down," Sam said. "You're losing it. And I can't have you blowing all of this right now, you hear me? If you bring too much attention on us, our whole operation will come crashing down."

"But—"

"No buts," said Sam. "Look, you enjoy your lifestyle, right?"

"What?"

"Do you like having fancy cars and a nice house and being able to basically do whatever you want all the time?"

"Well, yeah, but—"

"Me too. And the only reason we can do that is because your mom's family is rich," said Sam. "Which means we're rich, too. But only so long as I'm married to her. I signed a pre-nup. And if word gets out about... you know... that thing we've been working on... I'll be fired and then she'll have no choice but to kick me to the curb. And then I'm stuck cleaning washrooms or some shit. Do you have any idea how much a janitor's salary is?"

"No."

"I do. And it sucks," said Sam. "And if I'm out, you can be damned sure you're out, too. Do you wanna be thirty years old, living with your old man in a trailer, scrubbing toilets every day just so we can afford a can of beans for dinner?"

"No," said Bradley.

"Me neither," said Sam. "So for both of our sakes, pull yourself together, realize that it's not her, and that the dead don't come back."

"You don't understand!"

"I understand that you're going to screw this whole thing up. Now calm down. I think I know who's behind this. As soon as Kai is out of here, we're going to go deal with it."

"I already know who's behind it," said Bradley. "It's Rose! Rose is behind it! You know I'm right!"

"You shut your whore mouth," said Sam. "It's not her."

"You saw her!"

"I saw something," said Sam, taking his keys out of his pocket. "But it wasn't her. Now let's go figure this thing out."

"There's nothing to figure out," Bradley said, grabbing the keys and running. "And I can prove it."

"God damn it," said Sam, taking up after him. Blaine groaned and followed.

Bradley reached Sam's car and found all four tires flattened. Blaine's car was the same.

"What the hell?" Sam said.

Bradley turned, deked out Sam and Blaine, and ran up to a waiting ambulance. The driver was asleep, awaiting a call that was unlikely to come. Bradley pulled open the door, dragged the driver out, and dropped him on the pavement. He jumped in and took off, back doors open and swinging.

"Stop him!" Sam shouted.

The befuddled EMT just looked around.

"Radio for help!" said Sam.

"My radio's in the ambulance."

Sam swore and ran back into the hospital and up to

the triage desk.

"I need your radio."

"What?"

"Your radio. I need to radio the police."

"Sir, I'm going to have to ask you to—"

"Do you have any idea who I am?" Sam said, pulling out his wallet and showing his badge while running around behind the counter. "Now where's your—never mind, I see it."

Sam grabbed the radio and called out to Bradley, but there was no response. So he switched to the police band. "All units, this is Sheriff Wagner. Be on the lookout for a speeding ambulance. Unless its emergency lights are on, pull it over. And then call me. Do not engage. Keep the driver at bay until I arrive on the scene. I repeat: don't do a damned thing until I get there."

He slammed the radio down and said, "Now let's see who's responsible for all this. Nurse, where are your cameras?"

"Cameras?"

"Security. Your security cameras. Where are they?"

"Security office is at the end of the hall," said the triage nurse.

Without thanking her, Sam stormed his way down the hall, Blaine at his heels.

Twenty-Three

Bradley sped up the cemetery drive as the rain began to come down. He skidded to a halt largely aided by a huge oak tree. He jumped out of the ambulance and ran through the rows of headstones until he found the one he was looking for. He'd been there exactly once before, about three months earlier, and had barely given it any thought since. The stone was less weathered than the other ones. Engraved on the front were a pair of dates tragically too close together.

"What the hell do you want from me?" he said, kicking it. "Leave me alone! Do you hear me?"

A small stone structure stood nearby. It was adorned with ivy and had a heavy wooden door. He ran up to it and tried to open it, but it had a heavy padlock on it. He took several kicks at the door but succeeded only in injuring his foot. Using a large rock, he succeeded in breaking the lock and gained entrance to the structure. Inside was an assortment of gardening equipment; gloves, topsoil, trowels... and shovels.

He grabbed a shovel, ran to Rose's grave, and started

digging. It took all of about forty-five seconds for him to realize that a shovel wasn't going to cut it. He leaned on the shovel and looked around. In the distance, he saw another structure, similar to the garden shed, but much larger.

Bradley ran back to the dented ambulance as the rain began to pour. He backed it away from the tree, leaving the bumper behind, and floored it onto the grass. He sped between rows of stones until he crashed into the door. It cracked open. Half of the door crashed to the ground. The other half hung, squeaking, by one hinge. A pile of debris fell onto the windshield but, when the dust cleared, he saw what he was looking for: a backhoe.

He backed the ambulance out, climbed into the backhoe, and found the keys in the ignition. Knocking down the remaining piece of door, he ambled his way out into the yard and over to Rose's grave. It took him a couple of minutes to figure out the controls, but he soon had a gaping hole filling up with rain water and a pile of mud beside it. It wasn't efficient. It wasn't pretty, but it worked. As he dug, he heard a crunch and the next scoop brought up splintered pieces of a coffin. He dropped it on top of the pile of dirt and ran to the grave. In the hole was nothing but mud, rainwater, and broken casket. There was no body.

He cackled. "I knew it! It's her! It's actually her!"

Bradley pulled out his phone, looked up a number, and called it.

"Have I got a scoop for you," he said. "Pinelawn Cemetery isn't burying people. They're burying empty caskets. That's right. Yes, I can prove it. I'm there now. I dug up my ex-girlfriend's grave and she's not there. Yes. That's right. Yes, you heard me correctly. Her grave is empty. Get here ASAP, okay?"

Twenty-Four

"This is the one for the side lot," said Shawn Williams, the hospital security guard, holding up a video tape.

"You still use tape?" Sam said. "What kind of operation are you running?"

"One with serious funding cuts," said Shawn. "You wanna watch it or not?"

"Of course I wanna watch it, what the hell do you think?"

Shawn put the tape in, hit *Play* and then rewound it. Sam saw a flicker of activity around his and Blaine's cars, which suddenly sat higher off the ground. "There! What was that?"

Shawn stopped the tape, hit *Play*, and they waited. A figure appeared on the side of the road in the distance. A dark-haired girl in a white dress. Sam began to say something but she disappeared. She reappeared a fraction of a second later on the opposite side of Sam's car and then ducked down behind it.

"What the hell was that?" said Sam.

"Let me back it up," said Shawn, and he did.

"The tape is broken. It's missing time or something," said Sam.

"Nah, watch the time code," Shawn said, pointing to where it displayed in the bottom right corner. "It's smooth."

"How can that be possible?" said Sam.

"No idea," said Shawn.

The camera was situated high enough that they could just make out some movement near the back tire of Sam's car. Then the figure appeared at the edge of the woods in the back. She crouched down and poked around in the grass.

Blaine stepped up closer to the monitor. "Can you enhance this?"

"Jesus, Blaine, it's not CSI," said Sam.

"That can't actually be her, can it?" said Blaine.

"Of course it can't."

"Whoever she is, she shouldn't be messing with a man's car," Shawn said. "That ain't cool."

"How is she doing that?" said Blaine.

"Could she have somehow messed with the cameras?" Sam asked.

"I don't see how," said Shawn. "Besides, if she could do that, why not just erase the tape?"

"And you're sure it's not the tape screwing up?"

"Don't see how it could be," said Shawn. "But you got a forensics department or whatever that can figure that out, right?"

"Technically, yeah, but we can't exactly afford to hire the best and brightest around here," Sam said.

On the tape, Rose ran across the parking lot, carrying a handful of something from the edge of the forest. She spent some time near each tire. Then, crouching, she ran around behind the car and to the near side.

Kneeling, she pulled off the cap to the air valve and crammed something into it. She looked around, scanning the area for people, and for a moment her face was in clear view of the camera.

"Right there," said Sam. "Back that up. Pause it."

Shawn did so and there it was. Rose's face. Eyeless and mud-smeared but unmistakable.

"What the hell?" said Blaine.

"It actually *is* her," said Sam.

"Her who?" Shawn asked.

"Nobody you need to concern yourself with," said Sam. "In fact, don't you have some rounds to do or something?"

"Yeah, sure," said Shawn. "I didn't see a thing."

"You're damn right, you didn't," Sam said. "In fact, the more nothing you saw, the fewer speeding tickets you'll get."

"Works for me."

"But if I hear you *did* see something, tickets will be the least of your worries."

"Man, I wasn't even here," said Shawn, backing out of the room.

"I'm open to theories," said Sam.

"It can't actually be her," Blaine said.

"Of course it can't. And yet..."

"I'm at a loss," said Blaine.

"Come on, let's go talk to Miss Carter," said Sam. "She's obviously involved."

"How are we getting there?"

"I called a squad car. It should be here by now."

Twenty-Five

Having lights, a siren, and a total disregard for anyone's safety can get you anywhere you want to go in record time. About halfway to Port Langston, the rain began to come down hard.

Sam banged on the door of Katya and Vijay's place. "Police. Open up!" He banged a few more times and called out, "Open up or I'm breaking the door down!"

"You can't actually do that, can you?" said Blaine.

"Sure I can. Do you hear that?"

"What?"

"That cry for help coming from inside," said Sam.

"I heard it, sir," said Deputy Nabiesko, the officer whose car they arrived in. "I also think I smell marijuana."

"Oh, yeah," said Blaine. "I smell that, too. Definitely."

Sam banged on the door again and shouted, "You've got until the count of three before I—"

Vijay opened the door.

"Can I help you, Officer?"

"I'd like to speak to Miss Carter," said Sam. "Immediately."

"Can I ask why?"

"You know exactly why," said Sam. "Now shut the hell up and get her."

"I'm afraid I don't," said Vijay. "She's asleep. She's recovering from serious surgery and really shouldn't be disturbed."

"Get her. Now," said Sam. "And pray that your immigration papers are in order because I'm not done with you. Not by a long shot."

"I was born here."

"Sure you were," said Sam. "Your taxes, then. Your mortgage, your car insurance, everything. I will make your life a living hell."

"It's okay, Vijay," came Katya's voice from inside.

"You sure?"

"Yeah."

Vijay stepped back and Katya came to the door. "What seems to be the problem, Officer?"

"The problem is that someone who looks an awful lot like Rose Kaidan is messing with my son."

Blaine's phone rang. He looked at the call display and stepped back from the door.

"Messing how?" Katya asked.

"You what?" said Blaine into the phone.

"I think you know exactly how. And it needs to stop. He's been through a rough time. Rose was his fiancée, and she died tragically in a car accident. A. Car. Accident," he repeated, poking her in the chest with each word. "And now you're messing with his mind, pretending to be her and scaring the hell out of him. You don't think he's been through enough?"

"I'm sure I have no idea what you're talking about."

"Well, I'm sure you do."

"Uh... Sheriff?"

"Bad time, Blaine," said Sam.

"It's Brad," Blaine said. "He says her grave is empty."

"What? How does he know?"

"He dug it up."

Sam stared at Blaine for a moment, his mouth agape, his face lit alternately red and blue by the lights of the squad car.

"He what?"

"He also called the news."

Sam spun on Katya, raised an admonishing finger, and said, "This isn't over." He jumped in the squad car, Blaine and the uniform right behind him, and took off without waiting for Blaine to close the door.

Katya closed the door and walked into the living room. "You heard all that?"

"Yeah," said Rose. "And for the record, I was not his fiancée."

"I feel like that's not really the point right now," said Katya.

"I know. I just wanted to make that clear," said Rose. "Anyway, I guess I should get going."

"Where?"

"Back to the beginning."

Twenty-Six

Sam skidded to a halt, sideways, behind the Channel Fifteen News van. Anchor Jennifer Albert and her two-person crew on camera, lights, and sound were already halfway to the grave site, with Bradley leading the way.

"Bradley!" Sam called out. "Bradley, stop!" But Bradley didn't hear him.

Running backwards behind him, Jennifer spoke to the camera. "We're on the scene at Pinedale Cemetery where Bradley Wagner, son of Sheriff Sam Wagner and highly-regarded local law firm owner Penelope Simons-Wagner has apparently exhumed the grave of his deceased fiancée and found no body. He alleges impropriety amongst the workers of the cemetery."

"Right here," said Bradley, stopping and pointing into the grave but looking at the camera. "Where is she? Huh? Where is Rose Kaidan?"

The news team shone its light into the hole. Jennifer stopped and opened her mouth to say something, but fell silent.

Her crew stopped and shared a look between them.

Sam and Blaine rushed up to the side of the grave, Officer Nabiesko close behind, and gazed into the hole.

"Oh, shit," said Blaine.

"See?" said Bradley. "You see? She's not there! She's trying to kill me. She's trying to get revenge for—"

He was cut off by Sam clapping his hand over his mouth. "Stop," he said.

Bradley tried to speak, but his words were muffled by his dad's huge hand.

"Shut up," Sam hissed into Bradley's ear. "Don't say another word."

He spun Bradley around and, with his other hand, pointed into the grave. "Look."

Bradley looked down and saw, pale, eyeless, covered in mud, and partially submerged in rainwater, the lifeless body of Rose Kaidan.

Twenty-Seven

"Sheriff Wagner, how does it feel to arrest your own son?" Jennifer Albert asked on behalf of all the viewers of Channel Fifteen News.

"Not very good, Jennifer," said Sam, as he ushered Bradley into the back of the squad car. "But we don't play favourites here in Langston County. He may be my son, but he's still under arrest."

"Can you tell us why he did this?"

"He's been under a lot of stress since his fiancée died in a car accident," Sam said. "We'll be sure to get him the help he needs."

Rose and Katya watched the repeat of the news report while pulling down the Big Board and dropping all of the sticky notes in a box. Katya asked, "So you just laid there while they dumped all that dirt back on top of you?"

"Not all of it," said Rose. "Just enough to cover me up and then I blinked back here. Sorry about the mud in the hallway, by the way. I'll get that cleaned up today."

"Not a problem," said Katya, dropping the last card

into the box. "So what happens now?"

"Well, I've got to wait for him to get him out of jail, obviously."

"I thought sending him to jail was the whole point."

"No," Rose said, shaking her head. "It's not like he'll stay in there for long. And I have to hear him confess."

"Why?"

"I don't know," said Rose. "I just do. In the meantime, I have other work to do."

"And I have to destroy all this evidence," said Katya, closing up the box.

Twenty-Eight

At seven in the morning, Sam showed up with five officers and a warrant.

"Step aside, Miss Carter," said Sam. "We're going to tear this place apart until we figure out how you're related to the strangeness that's been going on."

"I'm not," she said as the officers pushed her aside and entered the premises. Rose had already blinked away and the barbecue was still warm from burning a pile of sticky notes.

"I suppose it's just a coincidence that you show up at the coroner's asking about Rose Kaidan at the same time as somebody starts harassing my son while pretending to be her."

"I don't know anything about that," she said. "Maybe your son's just got a guilty conscience."

"Why would he have a guilty conscience?"

But Katya knew better than to slander the Sheriff's son in front of him.

"No reason," she said.

"Uh huh."

The officers made short work of the house. They tore apart sofa cushions, overturned chairs, pulled up floorboards, and dumped the contents of drawers everywhere. All the while two officers stood, each on an opposite side of Katya, who sat on a kitchen chair.

An officer ran up the stairs from the basement, carrying a laptop computer. "Sir, I've found something."

"What is it?"

"A computer, sir."

"So?"

"It was hidden in the wall."

"Was it, now?"

"I've never seen that before in my life," Katya said.

"Fire it up," said Sam. The officer set it on the kitchen table and hit power.

"Now when I get into this thing, what am I going to find? Some kind of hologram-making software? Maybe with a specialized ghost-creation setting? Something like that?"

"Does that even exist?" Katya asked.

"If it does, we'll find out," said Sam.

"It's password protected, sir," said the officer.

"What's the password?" Sam asked Katya.

"I have no idea."

"Of course you don't," Sam said. To the officer he said, "Bag it as evidence. Then take her to the station and book her."

Twenty-Nine

Sam was feeling pretty good about himself as he drove home. The sun would be up in a couple of hours at most, so he'd get a little bit of sleep and then head back to the station. With Katya in jail, the Rose sightings would stop. And the security video would surely prove that the disturbances had been her all along. Bradley was still in custody but he wouldn't be for long. Just long enough for the local media to forget about him and move on to the next big thing. Then Penelope would use her legal clout to spring him. Between the two of them, if they greased the right palms and threatened the right people, he probably wouldn't even do any time.

As he came around a corner, his headlights illuminated a dark-haired figure standing at the side of the road in a dirty white dress. He zoomed past her faster than he could process what he was seeing.

"What the hell?" he muttered. He hit the brakes and backed up, but she was gone. Sam grabbed his flashlight and shone it around the area. Nothing.

He continued driving for a couple of blocks until he saw her again. Driving past, he got on the radio and asked if Katya was still in her cell.

"Nobody's signed her out," was the reply.

"That's not what I asked you," he said. "I want you to walk over to her cell and look at her. Get a positive visual identification."

"Yes, sir. Stand by."

Thirty seconds later, the response came. "Yes, sir, she's there."

And the girl appeared again, standing at the side of the road, her hair in her face.

Sam got out of the car and approached her.

"Now, you just hold it right there," he said. And she disappeared.

He spun around, pointing his flashlight in all directions, but she was nowhere to be found.

"Show yourself!" he called. "I am an officer of the law and you will comply!"

But she didn't.

He got back in his car and continued on. A few miles later, there she was again. This time, she stood in the middle of the road. He accelerated and aimed at her. But just before he collided with her, she disappeared.

Sam spun the car around and went back the direction he'd come from, but again there was no sign of her. He was about to give up when he spotted her up a road to the left. He swerved onto that road and floored it. She disappeared again. Sam screamed in rage and punched the steering wheel. Then he saw her again, up the road, standing off to the side. He stomped the accelerator and bellowed a war cry. This time he saw the hollows of her eye sockets before she vanished. A split second later he found himself in the ditch, the front end of his car wrapped around a tree and the airbag deployed.

Sam squeezed around the airbag and out of the car. He turned around to find Rose standing right in front of him.

"What did you do?" she screamed.

He pulled his gun but she had already disappeared. Once again, he scanned his surroundings, but found nothing.

He pulled out his phone and made a call. "Blaine!" he said. "I need you to come get me. I'm way east on Stone Road, and I'm on foot. Bring Kai."

He hung up and made another call, this one to the police station.

"Davis," he said. "Sheriff Wagner. You remember that call I made an hour ago reporting my squad car stolen? Sure you do. I spoke to you, specifically... Yeah, that's right. You must have forgotten to make a note of it. Do it now. Make sure you mark it for an hour ago, understand? Great."

He grabbed the flashlight and continued down the road, constantly scanning his surroundings.

"I know what you did," she shouted, her voice echoing from the woods. Then again from another direction and again from another.

Sam tried to point the flashlight in the direction from which the voice came each time, but by the time his eyes focused on the spot, it had moved.

The voice stopped. Dead silence surrounded him. His pulse roared in his ears. Sam took a step forward. Suddenly, she was right there in front of him. Close enough to touch. The pits where her eyes once were stared back at him, her neck twisted at an impossible angle. She slapped the flashlight out of his hand and it skittered across the unpaved road.

Sam pulled the trigger. The sound of the shot was deafening after the silence that had preceded it. But the bullet missed its mark. By the time he had reacted, she was already gone.

He took a step towards the flashlight. She appeared behind it and kicked it farther out of the way. Sam once again fired off a pointless shot.

He took another step towards it and he felt a wind at his back. Lips touched his ear and said, "Boo!"

He spun around, away from the flashlight, gun at the ready. But of course she wasn't there. The flashlight moved and went out. He turned back around and fired off three shots in the direction where it had been. He listened for the sound of a body hitting the ground, but it didn't come.

Pulling out his phone, he approached the area where the flashlight had been. It was no longer there.

He tried to use the glow from his phone screen to illuminate the road, but it didn't help much. Then it, too, got slapped out of his hand. He dove for it as she reappeared and he scooped it up mere milliseconds before she could grab it. Rose disappeared again and he shoved the phone down the front of his pants.

Now he was stuck alone, in near total darkness and silence with a next-to-useless handgun.

He stood, listening. He thought he could hear her rustling in the leaves. Or maybe it was the wind. Or an animal. Assuming there were any that hadn't been scared away by the gunshots.

Finally, Blaine arrived. Kai sat sideways in the back seat, his leg elevated and in a cast. Sam got into the front seat and said, "What the hell took you so long?"

"I got here as quick as I could," Blaine said.

"Take me to a church."

"A church?"

"Yes, a church. You know what a church is, right? Take me to one."

"Which church?"

"I don't care. Any church," Sam said. "The closest one. Now."

Blaine pulled the car around and headed towards town.

"You drove me home from the Mehta-Carter residence," Sam said. "About an hour and a half ago. After my car was stolen. We were never out here."

"Understood," said Blaine with a nod, followed by, "What the—" when his headlights illuminated Rose, standing in the middle of the road. He hit the brakes.

"Don't stop!" Sam said. Blaine drove towards her. "But don't hit her, either. It's a trap. She'll lead you into a ditch."

"Then I'm taking the long way," Blaine said. He started to turn the car around.

"There's no point," Sam said. "She'll be there, too. Just keep going." So Blaine drove straight towards her, and she disappeared.

"That can't be her," Kai said.

"It sure as hell looks like her," said Blaine.

"It's her," said Sam. "I know it can't be, but it is. Or something that used to be her. Or whatever."

"How is that possible?" Blaine asked.

"I have no idea, but I'm guessing she can't walk on hallowed ground. And maybe we can get some spells or holy water or something."

"Will any of that work?" Kai asked.

"I don't know," said Sam. "It's all I've got. I've never done battle with a dead person before. Unless you two have got any suggestions."

"I got nothin'," said Kai.

"The hallowed ground thing seems as good an idea as any," Blaine said.

He pulled into the first church they saw. It was an old

stone building on the outskirts of the oldest area of the city, between a residential area and an abandoned tanning factory on the Langston River. It was small and covered in ivy. A pilgrim graveyard lay in the east yard. Nobody new had been buried there in well over a century.

They pulled over to the side of the road, got out, and walked up to the church. As they approached, Rose came walking around the corner from the side of the building.

"So much for the hallowed ground," said Blaine.

"Ah, screw this," said Sam. He pulled out his gun and fired. Rose disappeared and reappeared behind them. The bullet tore a chunk off of the church door, and Rose kicked Kai in his broken leg. He screamed and fell. She disappeared again.

"But... How?" said Blaine.

His car started up. Rose hit the accelerator and flew down the road. She pulled off the side without stopping and crashed through a bush and off the cliff, into the river. Sam and Blaine ran up to the bank, Kai hobbling along behind on his crutches. They weren't surprised to find the car empty as it sank.

"Hang on," said Sam, putting his gun away and pulling out his phone. "I'll call a squad car to pick us up." But before he was able to enter his password, Rose appeared, snatched the phone out of his hand, and threw it into the river. While it was still airborne, she blinked behind Blaine, kicked him in the back of the knee, and pushed him off the cliff to join the car and the phone. She disappeared again.

Blaine swam hard but the current carried him downstream and across to the other side. Sam ran along the cliff, trying to keep up with him, hoping to find a branch or a way to cross or a large rock to step on.

Blaine dragged himself out of the water on the other side. He knelt and choked, coughing up river water. "I'm okay," he said.

Sam called out, "How's your phone?"

Blaine pulled it out of his pocket, examined it, and shook his head. "Not enough rice in the world."

"You got yours?" Sam asked Kai as he came hobbling up behind them.

"It's in the car."

As Blaine began to pull himself to his feet, Rose appeared, kicked him in the face, and blinked twenty feet away, into the woods.

Blaine swore and ran towards her.

"Blaine, no!" said Sam. But he didn't listen.

Sam pointed to the Tate Street bridge, about a hundred feet downstream. "Let's go."

"You go ahead," said Kai, indicating his crutches. "I'll catch up."

Blaine chased Rose through the woods, scraping himself on bristles and needles. The going was slow, as there were no paths and the moonlight was insufficient.

He soon climbed out of a ditch and found himself in the parking lot of the old tanning factory. It was a three-storey concrete monstrosity. Most of the windows had been smashed by drunken teenagers with rocks and guns.

She stood on the roof, at the edge, her dress flapping in the wind. Sam came running up the driveway.

"Blaine! Stop!" he called out. But Blaine was already squeezing his way through a well-traveled opening in the wall. Sam followed him inside. Decades of pigeons, bats, and rats had made a mess of the inside. The stench nearly made him throw up. He followed Blaine up a corroded metal stairway and out onto the roof. The exit to the roof was a corrugated metal box with a sloping top and an old rusted door. Sam found Blaine standing there, staring into the woods.

"Where is she?"

Blaine pointed to where Rose was sitting in a tree. Walking to the edge, Sam pulled out his gun and pointed it at her.

She appeared behind him and pushed him, but he was too heavy for her to move. He spun around, gun at the ready, as she appeared behind Blaine and pushed him towards Sam. Blaine knocked into Sam's arm and he inadvertently pulled the trigger. The bullet flew off into the woods. Rose had already disappeared again.

Blaine and Sam scanned the woods but she was nowhere to be seen. A knocking sound came from behind the door. Sam walked up, gun at the ready, and whipped the door open. Nobody was there. Rose appeared behind him and kicked him in the back of the knees. He tumbled down the stairs and again accidentally pulled the trigger. The bullet bounced off the corrugated metal wall of the exit. Rose slammed the door shut and braced it under the handle with an old piece of metal debris.

She appeared in front of Blaine and leaned into his face. "Why did you do it?" she asked.

"Does it matter?"

"Just tell me and all this ends," she said. "You don't even like him. You just want to stay on his good side because you expect he'll take over the firm when his mother retires."

Sam began slamming against the door from the other side.

"Seems like you've already figured it out," Blaine said.

"But with him in jail, you could take over the whole thing."

"I don't want to be responsible for it. I just want to control the person who is. And I definitely don't want to be on that asshole's bad side," he said, nodding towards the door that was about to burst open. "Besides, how long do you think he'd stay in jail for?"

"So you helped to cover up my murder."

He shrugged. "It was just business. You were already dead. It's not like I could bring you back."

"That's all I need to know," she said.

She touched his face and he screamed. Jagged lines of black grew out from her fingertips along his face. They smouldered and Rose could smell the stench of burning flesh. She pushed him backwards, towards the edge of the building. Sam made one last run into the door and came crashing through. Rose grabbed Blaine in a bear hug and stepped off the side. They both plummeted.

Sam ran towards the edge of the building but heard movement at the top of the stairway. He spun around and opened fire.

Kai screamed and fell backwards down the stairs as blood sprayed across the wall. When the banging and clattering stopped, he moaned.

Sam ran to the staircase. "Kai? Are you alive?"

"I need an ambulance!"

"Where'd I hit you?"

"In the shoulder."

"You're fine," said Sam.

He was startled by a manic cackle and spun around to see Rose standing on the edge of the building.

"You will die!" she screeched, pointing at him. "Just like Blaine!"

Sam raised the gun and she stepped backwards, off the side of the building.

He ran to the edge and looked down. There was no sign of Rose, but Blaine's body, his head blackened and smoking, lay motionless on the cement.

Kai hobbled up to the side of the building, blood pouring out of his shoulder, and looked down.

"Oh, shit," he said. "Is he dead? He's dead, isn't he?"

"Yeah, he's dead," said Sam. "The only useful one of the bunch of you and now he's dead."

"That's it," said Kai. "I'm out. I'm not doing this anymore."

"You can't be out. You're in. You're in this for good," Sam said. "The second she died and you didn't report it, you were involved."

"What are you gonna do? Arrest me? Put me in jail? Fine. I'll be safe from her in there. And you'll be in there with me."

"Look, Kai," said Sam, holstering his gun. "Blaine was your friend. Bradley is your friend. Do you wanna turn your back on your friend when he needs you the most?"

"Friends? They were never my friends," said Kai. "They just kept me around as an enforcer. They don't even really like me."

"Sure they do," said Sam. "Or did, in Blaine's case. All friendships are a business proposition. Some are just more open about it than others. You kept them safe, and they kept you in the good life."

"Well, I mean..."

"They paid for your steak dinners, your beers, bought you the good scotch... and the other stuff I'm not supposed to know about. Not to mention the women."

"Hey, Blaine paid for women," said Kai. "I can get my own for free."

"You sure about that?"

"Of course," Kai said. "I do okay."

"Yeah, I've seen some of the women you bring by," Sam said. "Like that one... who was that brunette? The one with the legs?"

"Samantha?"

"Samantha, yeah. She was a real looker, wasn't she?"

"Yeah, she was pretty hot."

"Too hot for you, I'd wager," said Sam.

"Yeah, that's what Blaine always said."

"You ever think there was a reason for that?"

Kai stared at him for a moment.

"Yeah," said Sam. "That one could act. Pretended she actually liked you and you weren't some 'roided-out freak. Blaine and Brad found her in Vegas. Remember that time you couldn't go? What was it? Your grandmother was sick or something?"

"My aunt."

"Your aunt," said Sam. "Right. Yeah, they found her down there. She was an aspiring actress who had taken up a different line of work. Blaine paid her stupid money to come up here for a couple of months to keep you company. Said you'd been a bit down, wanted to cheer you up."

"No," said Kai.

"I'm afraid so. But I mean, you had to have known that, right?" Sam said. "Deep down? A woman like that would never be with a guy like you. Would she?"

"But she..."

"Why was it she broke it off again?"

"She got a job in the UK."

"That's right," Sam said, "a job in the UK. Doing... what was it again?"

"You know... she never actually said. She was gone so fast."

"But she was going to email you, right?" said Sam.

"Said she'd keep in touch?"

"Yeah." Kai looked away, stared off into the forest.

"But it wasn't all bad, right?" said Sam. "You legitimately enjoyed yourself at the time. Even though you had to have known. And now you've got some pretty awesome memories."

"I guess," said Kai.

"And Blaine did all of that for you. I may have pitched in a bit, but the idea was all Blaine's," said Sam. "And here you are, claiming he wasn't your friend? He was. Maybe he wasn't at first, but he grew to like you. So did Brad."

"You think so?"

"I know so," said Sam. "Now, come on... The sun's coming up. Help me deal with the body quick and then I'll get you to a buddy of mine who deals with gunshot wounds."

"Shouldn't I get to a hospital?"

"Nah, you don't want to take a gunshot wound to a hospital," said Sam. "Too many questions. And by law they have to report it. I can only do so much meddling before it becomes too obvious."

"Okay," said Kai.

"Great," said Sam. "Now, let's get moving."

Thirty

A few hours later, sun came streaming through Sam's office window as he sat at his desk, trying to figure out what to do about the Rose situation.

"Sheriff Wagner?"

"Yeah, and you are?"

"Akib Hassan, sir. From IT. You had a special job for me?"

"Yeah, follow me," he said.

Sam led the IT guy down the hall. "I've never seen you before," he said.

"I'm new, sir," said Akib.

"You any good?"

"Well, I previously worked at Microsoft. Before that, I was at Apple, Uber, Pied Piper, Reynholm Industries—"

"Okay, okay, I don't need your whole resume," said Sam, leading him into a meeting room where a laptop sat on a table. "I just need to know if you can break into this thing."

"Sure, let me take a look," he said, and got to work.

"I need to know what kind of crazy crap is on there. Anything out of the ordinary."

"Like illegal hacking software?"

"Anything that'll let me keep the owner of it behind bars for the rest of her life," said Sam. "Or anything that can make live special effects."

"I'm sorry?"

"Honestly, I doubt that's even the issue at this point but I'll take anything."

"It just looks like a normal computer to me," he said.

"You're in already?"

"Yeah," said Akib. "It's a standard Windows laptop. Nothing exciting."

"Look closer. Search for anything even remotely questionable."

"If there's anything illicit on here, I'll find it."

"Good. See that you do," said Sam. "I'll be in my office. Come get me the second you find something."

"Yes sir."

"And you *will* find something, do you understand me?"

"I'm picking up what you're laying down, sir."

Sam stomped back to his office and checked for reports of a body found in the river near the old tanning factory. He knew the reports would never come. The body had been torn open, filled with rocks, and disposed of in a way that it was unlikely to ever be found.

Twenty minutes later, Akib arrived. "Sir?"

"What'd you find?"

"Nothing."

Sam stared at him for a moment. "I'm sorry?"

"Nothing, sir," Akib said. "I found nothing. It's clean. All the software is legit. There's nothing about special effects. No pornography. No pirating software.

Even the bookmarks are clean."

"I thought I told you to find something."

"I looked, sir, but there is nothing."

"Look again," he said.

"I've checked three times, sir," Akib said. "I'm sorry, but it's clean."

"I don't think you understand what I—"

"I understand perfectly," said Akib. "And I'm not going to plant something."

"I didn't ask you to—"

"You didn't have to. Your implication was clear. And I'm not doing it."

"You're fired."

"You can't actually fire me," said Akib.

"Maybe not, but I can fire the guy who can fire you," Sam said. "And I can make your life a living hell."

"You can certainly try."

"Your funeral. Now get the hell out of my sight," said Sam, standing up. "You'll want to get as far away from this city as possible."

Akib left the room quickly.

Sam picked up the phone and called Holding.

"Process Katya Carter," he said. "She's free to go."

Thirty-One

Two hours later, Vijay picked up Katya from the police station. Rose and Amar were in the back seat, trying not to be noticed in their sunglasses and ball caps.

"How's my hardened criminal?" Vijay asked.

"In need of a shower," Katya said. "Thanks for springing me."

"Don't thank me," said Vijay. "Thank Rose for causing a stir last night. And Amar for his social engineering."

"Don't thank me," Amar said. "Thank Akib Hassan."

"Who the hell is Akib Hassan?" Katya asked as Vijay started the car.

"I don't know," Amar said, holding up his counterfeit security pass. "But he's a good looking dude, don't you think?"

Katya laughed.

"Dude, Hassan is an Arabic name," Vijay said. "You do know that, right?"

"Yeah. And?"

"And you're Indian," said Vijay.

"You think that guy knows the difference?" said Amar.

"Did you do the accent?" Katya asked.

"Yeah, of course," Amar said. "I totally channeled Dad. Except I wasn't a continual disappointment to myself."

"You know you'll have to destroy that security pass, right?" Vijay said.

"Can I keep Akib's laptop?" Amar said, patting the backpack.

"No, you have to get rid of that thing, too," said Vijay, shaking his head. "If you're caught with that, you're screwed. And you can't leave it at our place. They'll come looking for it."

"Relax, bro," Amar said. "I've got a buddy who can take it for me. Or should I say an associate. But not a known associate, as far as the cops are concerned."

"As far as you know," Vijay said.

"It's cool. Trust me."

"I don't."

"That's okay," Amar said. "Katya trusts me."

Katya made a noncommittal noise, held out her hand, and tilted it in that "maybe" gesture.

"Rose? You trust me, right?"

"Honestly, dude, it doesn't matter. I have very little riding on whether or not you go back to jail," Rose said.

"Cold," said Amar.

"Yeah, well, I have a circulation issue."

"So what's up tonight?" Amar asked.

"I think I need to stay in tonight," Katya said.

"Me too," said Vijay. "It's been a stressful few days."

"It really has," Rose said. "By the way, I killed a guy. I just thought you should know."

"I'm sorry, what?" said Amar.

"I killed Blaine. Bradley's friend. Actually, 'friend' is stretching things a bit. He only hangs out with Bradley to further his law career. Hung out with," she corrected herself. "I guess he won't be doing that anymore."

"I'm really not comfortable with this," Amar said.

"I don't love it, either, I have to admit," said Katya. "But he really was a dick."

"Oh, my, yes," said Rose. "Also, he was there when I died, so..."

"Right," said Katya.

"Still," said Amar. But he didn't finish his thought.

"So yeah, you should probably go out tonight," Rose said. "To somewhere very public where you'll be recognized. At least for a bit."

"Why?" Katya asked.

"So you'll have an alibi."

Thirty-Two

Katya and Vijay stumbled home from the Shore Leave late that night after being sure to talk to as many people as possible. Their alibi was sound. Which didn't matter so much when Rose came crashing in the door a few minutes later, dragging Sam, unconscious and tied up with an extension cord.

"Help," she said.

"Rose, what did you do?" Katya said.

"I dropped a cinder block on his head."

"Ugh," said Sam.

"He's waking up," Vijay said.

"You two," said Sam. "I knew it."

"Quick, let's get him secured," Vijay said.

"No, let's dump him on his lawn," said Katya.

"We can't dump him," said Vijay. "He knows we're involved."

"I already knew," Sam muttered, groggily.

"I got him," Vijay said, and he took over Sam-dragging duties. Quickly, before he fully came to, Vijay dragged Sam to the basement and tied him to a chair in the old coal room.

"Wait, I thought you couldn't blink while carrying something," Katya said.

"I can't."

"So how far did you drag him?"

"Just from the car," said Rose. "Oh, by the way, I need to dispose of a squad car."

"On it," Vijay said, and he ran off.

Katya stood, staring at Sam for a few moments. He started to come to and struggled against his restraints.

"Why did you bring him here?"

"I'm sorry, I know I shouldn't have, but I need to question him."

"Rose, we don't bring douchebros home for questioning."

"But I need to know what happened," she said. "I need to know how they got away with it. And what other nefarious crap he's done. But mostly, I need to hear him admit it."

"I get it," said Katya. "I guess."

"You're got getting anything from me," Sam groaned.

"Admit it," Rose said.

"Admit what? That you're an idiot who fell for my even stupider son? That you were his latest momentary distraction?"

"I was more than that," she said. "At least at first."

"If you believe that, you're even stupider than I thought."

"Maybe you're just a bitter old asshole who married for money and upward mobility."

"And that's not what you were trying to do?"

"No!" she said. "I had no idea he had money when he asked me out. He just seemed like a nice guy. He was buying flowers for his mother."

Sam laughed at that, and then winced at the pain in his head. "Is that what he told you? Those weren't for his mom. They were for Charlotte."

"Who's Charlotte?"

"That big-titty one he told you was his cousin," said Sam. "Or was that Samantha? Desiree? I don't know, I can't keep track of his skanks. Either way, I can't believe you bought that line. God, you were so stupid. Blaine and Kai used to make fun of you when you weren't there. Sometimes when you were. Blaine did an absolutely spot-on impression of you. It was hilarious."

"Too bad you'll never see it again," said Rose and she hauled off and decked him in the face. Katya winced.

"That all you got, little girl?" he asked.

"You're lying."

"Am I? Ask him."

Rose furled her brow. If she'd had eye sockets, they would have narrowed.

"Well? Go on," Sam said. "Beam on out of here or whatever it is you do, find Bradley, and ask."

She glared at him, trying to figure out how much of what he'd just said was true.

"You can't, can you?" he said. "You can't get to him in jail. I wonder why that is."

"You want me to ask him?" Rose said. "Fine. I'll figure out a way." And she disappeared.

"Am I interrupting something?" said a voice from the doorway.

"Amar!" Katya said.

"Yeah. Hey," Amar said.

"Computer guy?" said Sam.

"I've got a little problem," Amar said.

"You've got a big problem now," said Sam to Amar. "I should have known you were in on this."

"Is this a bad time?" Amar asked.

"No, it's fine," Katya said, and she led him into the basement proper. "What's going on?"

"I've got a problem with a loan shark. Why do you have the county sheriff tied up in your basement?"

"Rose dragged him home to question him," said Katya. "You've been out of house arrest for, like, five days and you've already got a problem with a loan shark?"

"This is from before. He found out I'm a free man and he wants his money plus interest," Amar said. "Why can't Rose get into the jail? The cameras? I could disable them."

"No, it's because she can only go to places she's actually seen," said Katya. "How much?"

"I could break into the camera feed and show her that," Amar said. "Then maybe she can get in."

"Recordings don't count. It has to be with her own eyes," said Katya. "How much?"

"That sucks," said Amar. "I wonder if we can smuggle her in somehow."

"Seems unlikely," Katya said. "How much?"

"Well, if there's anything I can do to help..."

"How much, Amar?"

"A hundred and fifty thousand."

Katya blinked. "A hundred and fifty thousand what?"

"Dollars."

"Like, real, human dollars or some kind of weird cyber dollars?"

"No, real dollars," said Amar. "They took my Bitcoin rig in the raid."

"I'm sorry, Amar, but we don't have that kind of money."

"That's okay," he said, nodding. "I figured it was a long shot but I thought I'd ask. I should probably get going."

"Okay," she said, following him up the stairs. "I really am sorry, but after my medical bills we're on thin ice as it is. Plus we've got our own weirdness going on right now."

"You sure do," he said. "Thanks, anyway. I'll figure something out."

"If I can help in any other way, you know I will," she said as they reached the living room.

"I know. Thanks," he said, approaching the front door. "Where's Vij?"

"Disposing of a stolen cop car."

"Gangsta," he said, nodding approvingly.

Katya saw him out and went downstairs to try to figure out what to do about her unexpected guest. But the problem had solved itself. The chair back was broken, the ropes were on the floor and the window was unlatched.

"Shit!" Katya said. She jumped onto the chair and leaned out the window in time to see Sam disappearing over the back fence.

Katya took the basement steps two at a time and ran out the front door. Sam would likely go out through the yard of the house behind them and then he'd have to turn either left or right. She took a chance and went left, moving faster than she'd moved in a long time. She got to the end of the block, made another left, and ran almost directly into Sam coming the other way. She punched him in the face but succeeded only in hurting her own fist. Sam returned the punch and she fell hard on her back, knocking the wind out of her. Sam ran past her. Katya reached out and grabbed a rock from the garden beside her. She rolled to the side, jumped up, and threw the rock. It slammed into Sam's head with a crack and he went down hard.

Katya bent down, grabbed a stick, and ran toward him. Moaning, he rolled onto his back. Katya dropped to her knees beside him and raised the stick. He pulled his knee up and slammed his foot up into Katya's chest, lifting her off the ground and sending her sprawling. She hit her head on a rock and was out cold.

She awoke with a splitting headache, pulled herself up on her feet, and stumbled home.

"There you are," said Vijay. "I came home to find nobody here and Sam gone."

"He escaped."

"That's not good," Vijay said.

"I tried to chase him down but he knocked me out and got away."

"You what?"

"I had to do something," she said. "He knows for sure we're involved now."

"So he'll be back."

"That seems likely," said Katya.

"We need to get out of here," Vijay said. "Go somewhere he won't know about."

"But then Rose won't know about it, either."

"Yeah. I want to say Rose can take care of herself, but..."

"We can't just abandon her," Katya said. "Not now."

"I guess we wait for now," said Vijay. "For all we know, Rose is taking care of Sam as we speak."

"The same way she took care of that Blaine guy?"

"Yeah, well..." Vijay said. "Maybe? I don't know. And I'm not sure how I feel about that whole situation."

"Yeah, I know what you mean."

"She killed a guy, Kat."

"I know. But he killed her first," said Katya. "Or at least helped the guy who did."

"Yeah, but..."

"I know," said Katya. "But we're involved now. And at the moment we've got bigger problems. What if Sam comes back? And what if he brings reinforcements?"

"Well, what can they do? Nobody's going to believe that a woman came back from the dead. Sam tells them that, he's gonna end up in a padded cell."

"I feel like Sam doesn't need many reasons to do anything around here," Katya said.

They stood in silence for a moment.

"We've got to wait. At least for a bit," Katya said. "If Sam shows up, we run. We sneak out the back door. Otherwise, we wait for Rose. We at least have to let her know what happened."

"Agreed," he said.

Thirty-Three

Rose appeared in an alley by the police station. She walked along the side and around back. The fence would keep out most people, but not Rose. She blinked into the yard and walked around the back of the building. The wall was imposing and plain. There were no windows. It seemed the most likely area to keep the holding cells. But how to get in? If she couldn't see in, she couldn't enter.

She blinked back out to the side parking lot, walked around front, and went inside.

The duty officer didn't even look up from his fishing magazine when she approached the desk.

"Hello," she said.

"What can I do for you?" he asked, and glanced up for a brief moment. He did a double take and then said, "Are you okay, ma'am?"

Rose reached across the desk, took his fishing magazine, threw it aside, and slapped him.

A few minutes later she was behind bars, booked as Jane Doe. Her lack of eyes was cause for consternation but since she seemed fine otherwise, and refused medical attention, they let it go.

She was in one of three cells. Only one other was occupied, but it wasn't by Bradley. Instead, a woman lay snoring on a cot.

She blinked to the other side of the bars. At the end of the hallway was an imposing steel door with a sliding piece that functioned as a window. She was unable to slide it from her side. She banged on the door and called out.

"Excuse me," she said. "Officers?"

The slat opened up and a guard said, "How did you get out of your cell?"

"Never mind that," said Rose. "Where is Bradley?"

"What?"

"Bradley Wagner," she said. "I need to see him."

"Is that what this is about?" he said. Then to the other police he called out, "Guys, she's a groupie. Who had that in the pool?"

"Called it!" came a woman's voice from somewhere beyond.

"Janice wins it!" another voice called.

"That's three in a row," said the guard.

"I'm gonna keep this streak rollin'," said Janice.

"I'm not a groupie," said Rose.

"No, of course not. You're obviously his lawyer. A too-young, creepy-ass, eyeless lawyer," said the guard. "Listen, kid, I don't know what your issue is, but you've got to get some help for it, okay? Chasing after grave robbers? What the hell is that about? Now step back from the door, I'm going to put you back into cell."

"Fine," she said, and stepped back.

But when he opened the door, she was gone.

She didn't know Kai so well. He never spoke much and just seemed to be there as muscle. She wasn't even sure he and Bradley liked each other. She blinked around to their usual haunts; Jimbo's and Rollers first, but his car was nowhere to be seen. She didn't dare go in. She knew she could escape easily enough should anybody threaten her, but she didn't want to cause concern. Nor did she want news of her movements to get back to Sam and Bradley. She tried a few other places, restaurants Bradley had taken her to. The strip club on the edge of town that he claimed not to frequent. There was no sign of Kai anywhere.

She blinked out to the old tanning factory. The blood spatter from Kai's wound was already fading. Soon, it would just look like more rust. Blaine's body was gone.

She blinked to the top of the riverside bank and looked down. There was no sign of Blaine's car. She knew that the chances of him ever being found were practically zero.

Finally, she blinked to the graveyard. She sat down, her legs outstretched, her back against her headstone, and sighed.

She sat there for a good, long time, looking at the stars and racking her brain, trying to think of where they might be. Finally, she went home.

"There you are," said Katya. "Tell me you've stopped them."

"Stopped them? Stopped who?" she said. "Brad's still in jail and I can't get in to see him. And I have no idea where Kai is. Maybe Sam knows."

"He probably does, but that's going to be a problem," Katya said, and she related the evening's events.

"This is bad," Rose said.

"Very," said Katya. "We need a plan. I'm surprised Sam hasn't already come back for us."

"I think he has," said Vijay, pointing to the front

window, where orange lights flickered through the curtain.

"Are those cop car lights?" said Rose.

"They don't look like it," said Katya.

Vijay pulled the curtain aside to reveal flames. "Oh, shit!"

He ran to the door but Katya yelled, "Wait!" He stopped. "You don't just whip open a door during a fire."

"Also, it could be a trap," said Rose. "They could be out there with guns waiting for you to come out."

"Back door?" Vijay said.

"Hang on," said Rose and she disappeared. She returned a moment later and said, "No, they're long gone. But the fire's spreading fast."

"I'll call Nine-One-One," Vijay said, getting out his phone.

"No," Katya said. "Escape first. Then Nine-One-One."

"Okay," he said. "So what do we do? Just make a run for it?"

"It's our best chance," Katya said, and she approached the door. She opened it a crack but it wouldn't go any further. "It's chained shut!"

"Back door," Vijay said and they ran. Rose was already there, trying to pry it open.

"It's chained, too," she said.

"Window?" Katya said.

"Looks like they're melting," Vijay said.

"They must have sprayed gasoline on them or something," said Katya.

"Do you have bolt cutters?" Rose asked.

"No," Vijay said.

"An axe?"

"Yeah, but it's in the garden shed."

Rose disappeared and a few moments later a

pounding noise came from outside. It repeated several times until the door burst open, the chain hanging limply from a chunk of wood.

"Run!" Rose yelled, and they burst out through the flames and collapsed in the back yard. "Are you all right?"

"A little cooked, but I'm okay," said Vijay. "Kat?"

"Yeah," she said, nodding and panting.

Vijay pulled out his phone.

"Wait, you can't call nine-one-one," Katya said. "They'll know we survived. They can't know."

Hesitantly, Vijay put away his phone.

They climbed the back fence in the same spot Sam had and ran up the side of their rear neighbour's house to the street and around the block to their house. People were already standing out front and all along the street, watching in horror. Someone else must have already called emergency, as they could hear sirens come screaming towards them.

They stood, numb, staring at their home as it was devoured. All of their belongings, gone. The sofa, the TV, all of their books and music and movies. All of their clothes. The unused crib, sitting unmoved all this time, until the second floor gave out and came crashing down.

They stood in the back of the crowd, hoping to not be noticed by anyone they knew, but unable to tear themselves away. But one person noticed them.

"Well, well, well... I guess this is God punishing you for refusing to repaint that awful door."

Pamela Harrington suddenly found herself looking upwards at a circle of astonished faces, her jaw throbbing. Katya stood over her with a pained expression on her face, while she grunted and shook the pain out of her hand.

Thirty-Four

"Thanks, Mom," Katya said. "I didn't know where else to go."

Aileen Carter and Adrik Gagarin's house was modest but immaculately kept, with a lush garden and the liquor cabinet to end all liquor cabinets. Vijay was in the guest room and Rose was in the living room, laying on the sofa and pretending to sleep. Katya and Aileen sat in the kitchen, making use of the aforementioned liquor cabinet. Adrik was in his ersatz cottage in the basement—which was where he spent most of his time—pretending there weren't guests in his house. Especially not one who was a stranger.

"Of course, darling," said Aileen. "I'm so sorry about what happened. I can't believe it."

"I know. I'm still processing it."

"I can only imagine," Aileen said. "But you know you can stay here as long as you want. All three of you."

"I know. Thank you," said Katya, nodding. "But we won't be long. I promise."

"Take as long as you need, sweetheart. Again, all

three of you." Her left eyebrow rose in a suggestive manner.

"Thanks again," Katya said. "We really appreciate it."

"All three of you appreciate it?"

"Gee, Mom, are you trying to get at something?"

"I'm just a little surprised," Aileen said. "Not about you, so much, but Vijay. I didn't think he had it in him."

"What are you talking about, Mom?"

"Oh, please, dear. I wasn't born yesterday."

"She's our friend, Mom."

"Mmm hmm," she said. "Your father and I have had a few similar friends over the years. Which one of you actually picked her up? It was you, wasn't it?"

"Mom, it's not like that. Also, what?"

"Don't tell me you didn't know."

"Know what?"

"Amanda Dawkins," she said.

"Auntie Amanda?"

"Ah, yes, 'auntie.' Sure," she said. "That's what we said to keep the nosy neighbours off the scent."

"I'm sorry, what?"

"Surely you knew, darling," Aileen said. "Amanda was our girlfriend for years."

"What?"

"Your father actually found her, shockingly," she said. "I've found most of them over the years, but I've got to hand it to him, he picked up the best."

"You're joking."

"I am not," said Aileen.

"I can't believe what I'm hearing."

"You seriously didn't know?"

"No, I didn't know. How would I know?"

"Well, I'd just assumed you'd figured it out."

Katya just stared, her mouth agape. She still had no

idea if she was being punked or not and was waiting for her mother to drop the punchline.

"Well, if you think that's shocking, darling, I would advise you to not think too hard about Jim Campbell," Aileen said.

"Dad's camping buddy?"

"Camping? Please," she said. "Long weekends in New York City are hardly camping. Camp, perhaps, but not camping."

"Now I know you're joking."

"Am I, dear?" Aileen said. "Ask yourself this... Did you ever see them pack a tent?"

"Uh..."

"A sleeping bag? Shovel? Those little single-serving cereal packets?"

"Holy crap," said Katya. "How am I just learning about this now?"

"It's not like we kept it from you," Aileen said. "We just never explicitly spoke about it. Now... Tell me about the young lady sleeping on our sofa."

"Honestly, Mom, there's nothing to tell."

"Try again."

Katya knew she would never get any sleep until she gave her mom a satisfactory answer. "Fine, Mom, if you must know... She's dead. She's an organ donor and I got her heart when she died. So she came back from the grave to enlist my help in getting revenge on the boyfriend who killed her."

Aileen sat in silence for a moment. "Very well, then. Keep your secrets," she said, and she drained the last of her scotch. "Sleep well," she said, getting up and going to bed.

Thirty-Five

After waking up the next afternoon, Katya, Vijay, and Rose sat around Aileen and Adrik's living room. Adrik sat in his room in the basement watching his stories while Aileen was out with friends.

"So what do we do now?" Katya asked.

"You deal with insurance and such," said Rose. "And get to a new county, where that guy has no power. You're not safe here."

"We can't just leave you alone," Katya said.

"Well, I can't do anything until Bradley gets out of jail."

"Then I guess today's your lucky day," Vijay said, indicating the TV. He unmuted it just in time to hear Channel 15's Jennifer Albert explain that Bradley had been moved to an undisclosed location for his own safety after certain unspecified threats.

"I wonder where it could be," Rose said.

"A relative's place?" said Vijay.

"A different jail?" said Rose.

"What are the chances they've just taken him

home?" Vijay asked.

"I honestly wouldn't be surprised," said Rose.

"No, I suspect it'll be somewhere you've never been," Katya said.

"What makes you say that?"

Katya looked at Rose guiltily.

"Katya?"

"I think Sam might have heard me telling Amar about your... limitations regarding your method of travel."

"Aw, crap," Rose said, sitting back in her chair.

"I know," Katya said. "I'm really sorry."

"It's okay," she said. "I'll figure it out."

"How?"

"I don't know," said Rose. "But I've got until tonight to think about it."

"Why tonight?" Vijay asked.

"I'm way scarier at night."

Thirty-Six

Late that night, Rose blinked over to Bradley's place. His car wasn't there. There was no light coming from his window, so she blinked into his room. He wasn't there. She listened at the door and didn't hear anybody in the hallway, so she blinked out into the hallway and to the top of the stairs. She stood for a moment gazing down them. She blinked to the bottom and crept around the house, checking the living room and the basement den. He wasn't in any of his usual spots.

She blinked over to the roadside near Jimbo's. It was long-closed and dark. His car wasn't there, either. She blinked to the hospital parking lot, just in case it was still there but, as she suspected, it wasn't. It also wasn't at Blaine's place, or in the parking lot at his work.

She blinked back to the Wagner residence and carefully opened the door to his parents' room. Penelope lay in bed, asleep and alone. Sam was elsewhere. Probably wherever Bradley was.

She blinked back to Aileen's place and called the

police station's non-emergency line.

"Hi. Is Sheriff Wagner in, by any chance?"

"At this time of night? No, sorry. Is there anything I can help you with?"

She hung up and considered her predicament. Then she had an idea.

"A car is a place, right?" she said to herself. And she blinked into Bradley's car. Wherever it was, it was dark. As quietly as she could, she opened the door and got out, feeling her way around. The floor was cold and rough. Concrete? Maybe. She walked forward with her arms ahead of her until she found a wall. She felt her way along it and encountered a set of metal shelves where she promptly knocked down something heavy and it clattered to the floor. She paused and listened. Whatever it was, if didn't appear to have disturbed anybody. She continued on her way until she came to a staircase. She felt her way up and found there were only three stairs, leading to a door. Where there's a door, there's a light switch, she thought. And she was right. It took a moment for her to adjust to the light - something she found curious but wasn't going to worry about right then. She found herself in a four-car garage.

Bradley never parked his car in the garage, preferring instead to leave it where people could see and envy it. He must be taking the situation very seriously.

She eased the door open and peeked inside. The lights were off but she recognized the hallway as being inside the Wagner home.

She blinked outside, where she unscrewed the ancient landline. Then she appeared in Penelope's bedroom, where she was sleeping. She took Penelope's cell phone and snuck out to the washroom, where she dropped it in the toilet. She blinked to the kitchen and threw a chair against the wall, then stood silent and listened. Nothing. Two more chairs soon met similar fates. She flipped the table, opened a cupboard door, and threw a frying pan across the room.

She heard the bedroom door open upstairs and she stopped.

"Hello?" came Penelope's voice from the top of the stairs. "Sam?"

Rose blinked up to Penelope's room and slammed the door shut from the inside. She heard Penelope scream. Rose threw a table lamp against the door. Penelope screamed again and ran down the stairs. Rose blinked out of the bedroom and to the top of the stairs. She heard Penelope collide with something in the kitchen and fall down. A moment later the kitchen light came on and Penelope screamed again.

Rose took that as her cue. She knocked her neck out of joint and stepped forwards. Penelope came running out of the kitchen and into the front hall. She froze when she saw Rose descending the stairway. She pointed an accusatory finger and said, in her best croaky metal voice, "Where is he?"

Penelope ran back into the kitchen, where she was greeted by the same ghastly sight.

"Where is my killer?" said Rose.

Penelope spun around and ran back the way she had come, only to find Rose on the stairs again. She ripped open the front door, attempting to flee to her car, only to come face-to-horrifying-face with Rose, standing on the front porch.

"Give up your son or you will join me in death!"

"No!" Penelope howled and she dropped to her knees. "Please no! Please don't kill me. Please."

Rose leaned down to her and reached out her cold hand to stroke Penelope's cheek. Penelope shuddered, tears and snot running down her face.

"Where is Bradley?"

"I don't know," Penelope said.

"Tell me!"

"I don't know!" she repeated. "Sam has a place he takes his women. He thinks I don't know, but I do. It's somewhere out on the rural routes, I think. I don't know for sure. He's probably there."

Rose knelt down and placed her hands on either side of Penelope's head.

"One quick twist..." she said.

Kneeling there, Penelope took a deep breath and tried to regain her composure. She did her best to make eye contact with Rose's empty sockets.

"Please," she said.

Penelope Simons-Wagner felt a brief wind suck past her to fill in the sudden void in front of her. And she collapsed on the porch, crying.

Thirty-Seven

"The rural routes?" Katya said. "That's a lot of area."

"I know. Vijay drove me around out there for a few hours super early this morning but there was no sign of them anywhere."

"Apparently Rose trashed their cars," said Vijay, "so we were hoping to see an out-of-place squad car or something, but no such luck."

"Rose did what?"

"I thought it best not to ask."

"That may have been wise," Katya said. "But there's got to be a way to find them."

"Canvass the area?" said Vijay.

"What, just walk around and ask people if they've seen them?" Katya asked.

"Sure, why not?"

"That might raise too much attention," Rose said. "Besides, I'm sure they're laying low."

"Yeah, all that's going to do is scare them away," said Katya. "But even if you know where they are, what can you do? You can't get inside."

"I can if I can see in."

"They'll have thought of that, I'm sure," said Vijay. "They'll have hung up curtains or something."

"So I need a person on the inside," Rose said.

"That's not going to help you see in, though," Katya said. "It's not like one of us can go in and describe it to you."

"But I don't need to see it," said Rose. "As long as my eyes have."

"Wait... Are you saying what I think you're saying?" Katya asked.

"Someone out there has my eyes."

"But how are you going to find them?" Vijay asked. "They could be anywhere."

"They're somewhere chilly," Rose said.

"How do you know?" Vijay asked.

"Everyone there is wearing jackets," said Rose.

Thirty-Eight

The recipient of Rose's eyes walked past a small park just off a busy four-lane street.

Rose appeared in the park to the side of a bush just slightly taller than she was. She was aware of the fact that it was several degrees colder than the room she had just left, but it wasn't jarring like it would have been when she was alive. She was immediately struck by the smell of food. Something was very roasty and very garlicky. To her left, their front doors facing the park, were two Greek restaurants, side-by-side. She took a quick glance around. Nobody seemed to have noticed her appear out of nowhere.

Her eyes were headed west down the street. Rose followed them, keeping her eye sockets cast downwards whenever possible so nobody would notice that they were empty.

She passed a street sign written in English and another language she didn't recognize. Pedestrian traffic was not very heavy. She was in an older but well-kept part of town. Whatever town it was, she still didn't know. The streets were lined with shops and restaurants. She spotted three more Greek restaurants in close proximity.

Greek. That's what the language on the street sign was. She was in a city with a Greektown. Chicago? That didn't feel right.

She passed a discount store. Out front was a rack of clothing marked seventy-five percent off. She nonchalantly grabbed a coat on the way past and kept walking. She turned up a narrow alley, dropped the hanger, and slipped the coat on before she came out the other side, where she found herself on a residential street. It was an old neighbourhood with large houses set very close together. The coat was a bit large for her and she didn't love the particular shade of blue, but it would help her blend in much more easily. Now she just had to do something about her eyes.

She glanced into parked cars as she passed until she saw what she was looking for. A pair of dark glasses sat on a dashboard. Suddenly Rose sat in the driver's seat. She put the sunglasses on, got out of the car, and walked nonchalantly down the street.

She walked west to the next intersection and back south to the main street.

She passed a small group of mildly inebriated people laughing as they stumbled out of a restaurant, their exhaled breath materializing in small clouds around their heads.

Rose had no such cloud. She hoped nobody would notice.

She looked through her eyes and then down the street at the people walking ahead of her. Which one was her target? After a few quick comparisons, she was pretty sure she knew who it was.

The eye recipient appeared to be a woman about her

age, maybe a bit younger. She wore all black, including a short leather jacket and a vintage Sisters of Mercy t-shirt liberated from her aunt's closet. Her hair was dyed with purple streaks and she had meticulously-randomized holes torn in her fishnets, which descended into huge black boots adorned with non-functional buckles and zippers. She had a backpack with a Nine Inch Nails patch sewn onto it. So her musical tastes maybe weren't as heavy as Rose liked, but she figured they could get along.

The young woman turned and walked into a restaurant. To Rose's complete lack of surprise, it was Greek.

Rose continued walking while glancing through the woman's eyes. She saw the woman look around the restaurant until she spotted a woman with spiky pink hair sitting in a booth. She held a menu but was looking at Rose and smiling. Pink Hair stood as the eye recipient approached and they kissed. They sat and, although Rose couldn't hear them, they were obviously talking about the bottle of wine that Pink Hair had taken the liberty of ordering, along with two glasses.

They seem happy, Rose thought, and she smiled. She continued to walk down the street, past a book store, a vegan grocery, and a barcade, as the couple spoke and perused their menus.

She came upon a busy intersection. Straight ahead was nothing but traffic. The row of shops ended to make way for a four-lane bridge. She turned north and passed a subway station with a sign reading "Toronto Transit Commission."

I'm in Canada, she thought. *And I didn't even need my passport.*

She continued to walk as the area changed from restaurants and shops to apartment buildings and low-rise condos. To her right stretched residential streets lined with old, large, closely-packed houses. She turned down one of them as the server brought a plate of cheese that he set on fire and doused with lemon juice.

Rose wandered around the residential area, occasionally crossing the busy street with the restaurants, as the women followed up the cheese with souvlaki, more wine, baklava, and coffees. When the bill arrived, she made her way back to the restaurant. She arrived just in time to see them exit the restaurant and walk back the way the woman with her eyes had come from.

They walked right past Rose going the opposite direction. She saw herself through the woman's eyes, an experience which was only slightly disorienting.

When they passed her, Rose stopped and turned. She followed them along the street for a block and a half, then picked up her pace and sidled up to the dark-haired woman.

"Excuse me," said Rose.

"We don't have any change," said Pink Hair.

"What? Oh... no, I'm not..."

Pink Hair stopped walking and turned to Rose. "Jesus?"

"What?"

"Are you about to tell us all about your friend Jesus and how he changed your life?"

"No, I just..." Rose turned to the dark-haired woman. "I wanted to ask you about your eyes."

"My eyes?" said the eye recipient.

"They're not yours, right?" said Rose. "They were donated."

"Uh... yeah," said the woman.

"How could you possibly know that?" asked Pink

Hair.

"Okay, well, I know this sounds crazy, but..." said Rose. "Look, just don't freak out, okay?"

"Freak out about what?"

"It's just... look, I'm not here to hurt you, okay?" said Rose. "I just want to get that out of the way first. The last person I talked to about this got a little freaked out. Okay, a lot freaked out. But we're friends now. I guess. I mean, she's helping me with something. A very important project."

"Look, we're very busy people," said Pink Hair. "Can you maybe get to the point?"

"Right, sorry. It's just... your eyes?" Rose said. "They're mine."

"I'm sorry?" said Dark Hair.

"Well, they used to be."

"Let's go," said Pink Hair, and she started walking.

Dark hair moved to follow her and Rose said, "No, wait, look."

She pushed her sunglasses down to reveal her empty sockets.

"You have my eyes," she said.

The looks on the women's faces went from mild annoyance to confusion to fear in less than a second.

Pink Hair put her hand on the other woman's back and pushed her gently.

"Cecilia, run," she said. Cecilia ran.

Pink Hair punched Rose hard in the face, knocking her down. Her sunglasses went flying.

"Stay away from us!" said Pink Hair, wagging a finger at her, and she ran off after Cecilia.

Passing pedestrians either stared or pretended not to notice as Rose scrambled for her sunglasses and put them back on, hoping that nobody would realize she had no eyes.

"Are you okay?" said a passing pedestrian who tried to help her back to her feet.

"I'm fine," she said, shrugging him off and standing. She quickly walked in the direction her eyes had gone and ducked into a doorway.

She looked though her eyes and saw that they had stopped running, but Cecilia kept looking back. Rose was nowhere to be seen. Until Cecilia turned her head forward again.

"I think we got off on the wrong foot," said Rose, her coat and sunglasses now laying in a doorway half a block away.

Pink Hair grabbed Cecilia by the arm and pulled her onto the street. Dodging traffic, they crossed the road and kept running. Rose just watched them go.

She went back to the doorway and grabbed her liberated things. She wandered down the street while Cecilia and Pink Hair took a circuitous route through back streets and a park, crossing the main street twice, until they emerged from a back alley on a side street. They walked out to the main street and looked around for Rose, but she was blocks away, walking in the opposite direction. Pink Hair pulled out her keys and they hurried to a door beside a pub. Inside, they climbed two flights of stairs and entered their apartment.

"Finally, we're safe," said Pink Hair.

"I'm still not convinced she was dangerous," said Cecilia.

"She wanted to take your eyes!"

A knock at the door startled them both. Blocks away, a coat and a pair of sunglasses fell to the ground. Pink Hair looked out the peephole to see Rose, smiling and waving.

"Hi," she said. "I just want to talk."

Pink Hair covered the peep hole with her hand and spun around to Cecilia. "It's her!"

"What? How?"

"Go away!" Pink Hair shouted. "I'm calling the police!"

"Okay," said Rose.

Pink Hair watched her turn and walk down the stairs. She sighed and turned to Cecilia. "She's gone."

"How did she find us?"

"I have no idea."

"Because I can see through your eyes," said Rose.

Cecilia and Pink Hair screamed.

"Please hear me out," said Rose.

Pink Hair took a swing at Rose, who was suddenly behind them.

"I promise I'm not here to hurt you."

"How did you..." said Pink Hair, pointing alternately between where Rose was and where she had been.

"I don't know," said Rose.

"Well, you're not taking her eyes!"

"You're right, I'm not."

"You're not?" said Cecilia.

"I don't need them. I can see fine," said Rose. She pointed at things around the apartment and commented. "Your hair is pink. That wall is yellow. You need to take out your recycling. See? I'm good. Lovely apartment, by the way."

"But how...?" Cecilia began.

"I don't know. Look, let me start again... Hi. My name is Rose. Rose Kaidan. I was murdered by my dickbag of a boyfriend and his police chief father covered it up. My organs went to a bunch of different people. You got my eyes. Which is totally cool. You seem very nice and I'm glad to help since I don't need them any more. But I've returned from the grave to get revenge on those who've wronged me and I need your help. If you say no, that's fine. But please hear me out. I just need two minutes of your time."

"I'm sorry, did you say you were murdered?" said Cecilia.

"Yeah," she said, holding out her arm. "Feel my pulse."

Cecilia touched Rose's wrist. "You're cold."

"Yep. Permanently."

Cecilia repositioned her fingers a couple of times and said, "There's no pulse."

"Let me see," said Pink Hair. She put her hand on Rose's neck. "You *are* cold. And she's right, you have no pulse. How can you have no pulse?"

"Because my heart is in a woman named Katya Carter," said Rose. "She and her husband are helping me out with my revenge, as well. They're very nice people."

"I'm sorry, what?" said Pink Hair.

"Let me show you something," Rose said, and she pulled down the front of her dress to reveal her scar. "That's where they took my heart out."

"Oh, God!" said Cecila.

"It's okay, it's in someone who needs it."

Pink Hair inhaled sharply and pinched the bridge of her nose. "All of this is impossible," she said.

"That's what I would have thought just a few months ago," Rose said. "But here I am."

"You can't be."

"I know. I also can't see without eyes, but I do. And it's also impossible for me to just disappear and reappear in a different place, but you saw me do it."

"This is a lot to take in," said Cecilia.

"Oh, I know. Believe me, I know. But I got used to it and I'm sure you will, too."

"I can't even with this," Pink Hair said.

"Look... sorry, what are your names?"

"I'm Cecilia. Cecilia Zhang. This is my partner, Lori Wilson."

"Hi," said Lori.

"Lori, Cecilia... can we sit? I'd like to tell you about what's happened to me the last few days."

"Of course," said Cecilia. "Please, have a seat."

"I think I'm going to need some more wine," Lori said.

Rose spent the next hour telling them everything that had happened, from her hazy memories of walking all night though the rain, to accidentally scaring Katya out of her wits, to how they figured out how her powers worked. How her memories came back and how she gradually terrified Bradley until he'd gone into hiding.

"So that's where you come in," she said. "I need you to get in good with Bradley so I can see where he is."

"You want her to get in good with the guy who killed you," said Lori.

"Yes," said Rose.

"You want her to get pretend-involved with a murderer."

"Yes."

"Who killed you."

"Yes. But he started out nice," said Rose.

"They always do," Lori said.

Cecilia nodded and said, "I'll do it."

"You will?" said Rose and Lori at the same time.

"On two conditions: one... if I even suspect he's going to hurt me, I'm out."

"Of course," Rose said.

"Two... you don't look through my eyes unless you absolutely have to. They're mine now."

"Agreed," said Rose. "I suspect you won't need to

worry about that for too long, anyway."

"What do you mean?" Cecilia asked.

"Just a gut feeling," said Rose. "Anyway, if we can call Katya and Vijay, they'll make sure you've got a plane ticket waiting for you tomorrow. Is that cool?"

"Sounds good."

"Please tell me you have a passport."

"I do," said Cecilia.

"You're not actually doing this," Lori said.

"I think I have to."

"You absolutely do not," said Lori.

"Lori, you're always talking about wanting to improve the world, right?" said Cecilia. "You want to end suffering, hunger, hate?"

"Of course, but..."

"That's why we go to all those rallies and protests, right? That's why we volunteer at the food bank and donate to women's shelters."

"Well, yeah..."

"Lori, that's all great stuff and I'm always so proud of the work you do, but I have a chance here to help out one person in what might be a very profound way. I have to do it."

"What about your job?"

"I'm owed some vacation, remember?" said Cecilia. "Dave said I could book it any time, but I'd been saving it for something special. This is that something special."

"I thought our trip to Niagara Falls was going to be the something special."

"Yeah, because that's better than helping out someone in need and not selfish at all," Cecilia said.

"You're right, of course," Lori said, throwing up her hands in defeat. "Okay. If you're sure."

"I'm sure."

Lori nodded. "Right, then. I'm trusting her safety to you," she said to Rose.

"I'll return her in one piece, I promise."

"You'd better," said Lori. "If anything bad happens to her, I swear, I'll kill you."

She realized what she had said and the trio looked at each other awkwardly for a moment, and Rose began to laugh. Cecilia and Lori joined in.

Thirty-Nine

"Hey, Kat. I'd like you to meet my new friend Cecilia Zhang."

She handed Cecilia the phone.

"Hello?" she said.

"Hi, Cecilia, I'm Katya. Apparently you've met Rose."

"Uh... yeah," said Cecilia.

"So she's explained to you what's going on?"

"She has. There was a pretty interesting demonstration."

"Yeah, that's one word for it. So are you up for helping?"

"I guess," Cecilia said. "I mean, I'm pretty freaked out, I'm not gonna lie. But I can't argue that something weird is up."

"Believe me, I understand."

"I mean, she's obviously dead," Cecilia said. "She let me check her pulse and she doesn't have one. Not in her wrist, not in her neck."

"That's because I have her heart," said Katya.

"So she told me. And I'm no doctor but I've got a

pretty decent grasp of how important a heart is," said Cecilia. "Also, she can see without eyes. Which, I have to admit, is a bit creepy. But kind of awesome."

"You get used to it," said Katya.

"Really?"

"No, not really."

"But she's actually dead," said Cecilia.

"Ish," Katya said.

"And this Bradley guy killed her?"

"He did."

"Well... let's take him down, then."

Forty

The next evening, Rose, Katya, and Vijay picked Cecilia up from the airport, having flown in on Vijay's dime.

"Hey, Kat," said Rose, from the back seat. "Do you think we can take Cecilia out for a new outfit?"

"Sure. Vijay and I are going to need new wardrobes anyway, since ours burned up," said Katya.

"Good, because he is not going to go for this look."

"Why not?" Vijay said. "I think she looks cool."

"He's not into the Goth thing. Nothing alternative," Rose said. "He only wants girls that will impress his friends."

"I thought you were a metalhead," said Vijay.

"I mean, I like the music," Rose said. "But I never really dressed the part. Not in a town like Port Hackett. I didn't want people looking at me like I was a freak. No offense."

"None taken," said Cecilia. "I revel in it."

They filled Cecilia in on the details and discussed the plan on the way to Katya's parents' place, with a stopover at the local mega-chain cheap clothing retailer, where they bought a few outfits for Cecilia. She didn't even attempt to hide her disdain for the pastels.

"Just think of it as going undercover," said Vijay. "Like a spy."

"James Bond wore a cool white tux," she said. "And he had a Lotus that drove under water."

"That thing was so cool," Vijay said.

"Right? But I can do this," said Cecilia. "I can wear pastels for the greater good."

"They will sings songs of your heroism down through the ages," said Vijay.

They made a quick stop-off at their temporary home, got Cecilia into her costume, and showed her pictures of Bradley, Sam, and Kai. They avoided mentioning Blaine. Then they drove out to the rural routes and got to work.

The cottages were few and far between. Some were well-lit, windows open and fairly bustling with activity. Families having late barbecues, small groups of friends drinking. They gave those a miss and instead concentrated on the ones that were quiet or even appeared abandoned.

Vijay would park the car out of sight and Cecilia would knock on the door.

"Hi. I'm looking for Carrie? Carrie White?" she would say. "Am I in the right place?"

When she inevitably was not, she would apologize and move on. Vijay kept careful notes of where they had been on his map app.

They continued on until well after dark before they decided that it was getting too late to annoy people. The next morning, Vijay went to work and Katya called in sick again to take up driving and mapping duties. Rose sat quietly, watching through her own eyes.

Late that afternoon, Cecilia knocked on the door to a cabin that appeared to be abandoned. But the drapes ruffled and an eye peeked out.

"Hello?" she said.

The door opened slightly and she recognized the face that looked back at her. It was Kai.

"Can I help you?"

"Hi. I'm really sorry to bother you but I just moved in down the road and I can't get this bottle of scotch open," she said, holding up a bottle unknowingly donated to the cause by Aileen.

"Scotch?" he said, raising an eyebrow and opening the door a bit wider. He leaned awkwardly on a crutch with his right arm. His left arm was in a sling.

"Yeah. It's a really nice Islay single malt," she said. "I bought it to celebrate being newly single and now I can't get it open. I was hoping to find somebody with big, strong hands who could open it for me. I could pay you back with a shot of it if you want. Do you like scotch?"

"I do," said Bradley's voice from inside. He pulled the door open wider. "Is that a 22-year-old?"

"Yep, same as me," she said, giggling. "I'm curious if its legs are as good."

Bradley took a quick glance around behind her to make sure he wasn't being watched. "Only one way to find out. Come on in."

She followed them into the cabin. The inside was overwhelmingly brown. Everything was made of wood and it smelled musty. Dead animal heads adorned the walls. The only modern accoutrements were a giant TV and a selection of video game consoles. Some sort of first-person-shooter was paused in the middle of a headshot. There were two doors on the opposite wall and another to the left. To the right was a doorway leading to the kitchen. Bradley went through that doorway while he spoke.

"I'm Bradley, by the way," he said, taking three glasses out of the kitchen cupboard. "Bradley... uh... Smith. Bradley Smith. And this is Kai... Jones."

"Nice to meet you, Bradley Smith and Kai Jones," she said, handing Kai the bottle. "I'm Carrie. Carrie White."

"I'll get that," Bradley said, taking the bottle from Kai. He opened it and poured three glasses of scotch. They tapped glasses and each took a sip.

"Fantastic," said Bradley, who couldn't have differentiated it from a glass of llama piss but knew that it was expensive.

Cecilia heard the sound of a car crunching down the stone driveway.

"Wow, yeah, this is great," Cecilia said, nodding. "You know, I've gotta say... I wasn't sure who I'd find in the middle of nowhere like this. I was worried I might end up in a pit putting lotion in baskets. I'm glad I found someone cool."

"Oh, well, thanks," he said. "I'm glad I found someone cool, too."

"And cute," she said, and she took another sip, grinning.

"Did you say you're recently single?"

"I did," she said. The door opened and Sam walked in. He stopped and stared at her.

"Who the hell is this?" he said.

"This is Carrie," said Bradley. "She's staying just down the way."

"Hi," she said and extended her hand.

He ignored her, walked right past her, and grabbed Bradley by the arm. "Get in here," he said. "You too," and he led Bradley and Kai into one of the other rooms. The quick glance Cecilia got of the inside revealed it to be a bedroom.

Standing in the main room, she could hear their entire whispered conversation.

"What the hell do you think you're doing?"

"What? She's fine."

"You don't know that," he said.

She tiptoed to the other door and opened it as they continued to argue. Inside was another bedroom, but there was also a desk with an old style desktop computer. Mounted on the wall was a corkboard with a map of the area. Various coloured push-pins were stuck in it.

Sam uttered the words, "That's final," and the door was wrenched open.

"What the hell are you doing?" he said, and he pushed her out of the way.

"I was just looking for the washroom," she said.

"Well that isn't it," he said, getting too close to her and pulling the door shut. "You need to go. Now."

"Whatever. I didn't mean to intrude," she said, rolling her eyes.

"Dad, chill," said Bradley, coming out of the bedroom. "She's just a vacationer. She brought scotch."

"I don't care if she's the Queen of France and she brought God himself," Sam said. "We're supposed to be... having father/son bonding time. You know how important it is to your mom."

"Yeah, but..."

"No buts. She's leaving," he said. "What kind of young lady just takes a bottle of alcohol to a stranger's cottage, anyway?"

"I'm sorry. I'll be going," she said, picking up the scotch.

"Leave the bottle," he said.

Had she not been undercover, there would have been no way that would happen. Instead, she sighed, put the bottle down, and walked toward the door.

"Wait," Sam said. "Stop right there."

She stopped and turned. Sam walked into the room with the corkboard. He returned a few seconds later and said, "Fine. Go."

She left the cottage and walked back to the car. She heard the argument escalate but couldn't make out specifics.

Only Katya was in the car when she returned.

"I understand that was the place," said Katya.

"They certainly looked like our guys," said Cecilia.

"Rose said it was them, yeah," Katya said. "She's gone to do some reconnaissance or something."

"They're definitely up to something. They've got a War Room."

"I'm sorry?"

"There's a room with a Big Board with a map and pins and stuff," said Cecilia. "And that Sam guy was quite adamant that I not go in."

"Well, that's something," said Katya. "We need to get a better look at that room."

Rose appeared in the back seat. "Great job," she said.

"Thanks," said Cecilia. "You saw the War Room, I take it?"

"I did," she said, nodding. "And there's a flash drive that's super important to them."

"How do you know that?"

"Because I was in the other room when they kicked you out."

"So it worked," said Katya.

"Yep."

"Cool," said Cecilia.

"Let's drive around for a bit," Rose said. "I have an

idea."

"I can't wait to hear this one," Katya said.

They returned about an hour later. The sun had gone down and Sam's car was gone but a light was still on inside the cottage.

"Are you sure you're cool with this?" Rose asked.

"Yeah, of course," said Cecilia. "This is gonna be awesome."

Cecilia got out of the car and approached the cottage. Katya and Rose drove off to find an inconspicuous spot to park the car.

"Hello?" Cecilia said, knocking on the door. "Bradley? Are you there?"

Bradley peeked out the window, smiled and opened the door.

"Carrie. I was hoping you'd come back."

"Is your dad gone?"

"Yeah. He'll be gone a while."

"Cool," said Cecilia. "Did he leave us any scotch?"

"Yeah, come on in," he said.

"Where's your friend?"

"He went with my dad," said Bradley. "They've got some business to attend to."

"Just us, eh? Cool."

She entered and made herself at home on the sofa while Bradley poured two more drinks. He joined her and said, "I'm glad you came back. A lot of people are intimidated by my dad."

"Oh, please," she said. "What's he gonna do about it?"

"Right?" said Bradley, laughing.

"I mean did you hear him judging me for even being here?" she said. "Like maybe you're dangerous or something. Are you dangerous?"

"Me? Dangerous? Of course not."

"Please. You're, like, the farthest thing from dangerous."

"I know, right?" he said, laughing.

"I mean, what are you going to do? Kill me? Please," she said, laughing along with him. "You don't have it in you."

But his laughter stopped. He stared past her, wide-eyed.

She turned to follow his gaze. Rose stood on the other side of the room, pointing at him. "Murderer!" she screeched.

"What?" said Cecilia. "What's wrong?"

"Don't... don't you see her?"

"Who?" she said, innocently.

"Her!" he said, standing and pushing his back up against the wall.

"There's nobody there," said Cecilia.

Rose took another step forward and touched Cecilia gently on the upper arm. Cecilia screamed and stiffened. Her eyes rolled back into her head. She went silent and sank to the floor.

Bradley ran into the bedroom and slammed the door shut. Rose screeched and slammed on the door repeatedly while Cecilia got up, poured the scotch back into the bottle, and put it and the glasses back where they were. She grabbed Bradley's phone, snuck outside, and threw it as far as she could into the woods. As soon as Cecilia was gone, Rose blinked away, leaving the cottage silent except for the sounds of Bradley whimpering from under the bed.

Cecilia waited and listened at the door until she heard Bradley moving around inside. She knocked on the door.

"Bradley? Are you in there?"

Brad peeked out the curtain, his eyes wide. "Cecilia?"

"Yeah. Is your dad gone?"

Bradley opened the door, stuck his head out, and looked around, furtively.

"You're alive?"

"Of course I'm alive," said Cecilia. "Why wouldn't I be?"

"She... She killed you."

"What are you talking about?"

"Rose," he said. "I thought she killed you."

Cecilia looked at him quizzically. "Are you high?"

"What? No!"

"Don't tell me you drank all that scotch."

"No, just a couple sips," he said. "And whatever you had."

"I didn't have any," she said. "Your dad gave me the bum's rush before I could, remember?"

"No, I mean just now."

"Just now?" Cecilia said. "I just got here. Are you feeling okay?"

"But you just... You were here and she killed you."

Cecilia gave him an appraising look and asked, "Were you asleep?"

"What?"

"Were you having a nightmare?"

"No, it happened. You were here and Rose appeared and she touched you and you just... died," he trailed off, furrowed his brow, and looked at the floor.

"Funny, I don't remember being killed," said Cecilia. "Look, you obviously had a nightmare. How about you let me in and give me some of that scotch and tell me about it."

"Uh, sure," he said. "Okay." And he stepped back.

Cecilia sat in the same spot on the sofa while he poured two more drinks, his hands shaking. He sat down beside her and took a gulp.

"Whoa, easy there, tiger," she said. "Save some for later."

"Right, right," he said, and he took a deep breath.

"Now tell me about this nightmare," she said.

But instead of that, he pointed at Rose and screamed.

"What's wrong?" Cecilia asked.

Rose pointed at Bradley and croaked, "Give me the flash drive."

"It's her!" he said. "Right there!"

"Dude, there's nobody there."

"Give me the flash drive and the time loop will stop," she said.

"Time loop?" he said.

"Time loop?" Cecilia said. "What are you talking about?"

"Give me the flash drive," said Rose. "Or you will be forced to see your friend die over and over... Forever!"

"I can't," said Bradley.

"You can't what?" said Cecilia, as Rose touched her again. For a second time, she collapsed on the floor.

Rose reached out to Bradley, who once again ran into the bedroom. Rose kept up her shrieking routine while Cecilia reset the scene, including backing up the clock on the stove. When she was gone, Rose blinked back to the car where she sat and laughed for a good two minutes.

Cecilia knocked on the door again.

"Go away!" said Bradley from inside.

"Bradley? It's me, Carrie," said Cecilia. "Is your dad gone?"

"I said, go away!"

"Did he leave us any scotch?"

She heard Bradley scream and knew that Rose had blinked her way into the cottage. She opened the door to see him run into the bedroom.

The bedroom door opened and the drive flew past Rose and skidded across the floor.

Rose whipped open the door to the bedroom.

"Remove your pants!" Rose said.

"What?"

"Remove your pants!"

He pulled them off and flung them to the side of the room. Rose blinked directly behind him, put her mouth to his ear, and whispered, "Run."

He did.

"Dude, what are you doing?" Cecilia said.

"Run into town," Rose screamed. "Do not stop until you get home."

Rose held back her laughter until he disappeared around the corner. Cecilia joined her in laughter. "That wasn't in the script," she said.

"Last minute improv," said Rose.

"Inspired."

"Thanks," Rose said, retrieving the drive.

"No problem," Cecilia said, retrieving the scotch.

They proffered their spoils as they approached the car.

"You retrieved the bottle, too?" said Katya. "Nice."

"Side quest," Cecilia said. "Achievement unlocked."

Forty-One

Vijay, Katya, Rose, and Cecilia stepped off the creaky old elevator on the fifth floor of a brown and beige apartment building. The carpet was old and stained and about a third of the lights were either out or flickering. The hallway smelled like a mixture of feet, wet dog, and cabbage soup.

Vijay knocked on a door. The peephole darkened for a moment and then the door opened to reveal Amar. "Dude, what's up?"

"This is," Vijay said, holding up the flash drive.

Amar took a quick look down the hallway in both directions. "You're sure you weren't followed?"

"Positive."

He let them in. His apartment was extremely lived-in. He had obviously been sleeping on the sofa. The door to the bedroom was open, revealing his special effects workshop, which spilled out into the living room and the kitchen. Alien and monster heads stared back at the group around shimmering, futuristic swords and silver laser guns.

"This place is cool," Cecilia said, nodding approvingly.

Vijay introduced Cecilia to Amar and gave him a brief explanation of who she was.

"So what's on the drive?" said Amar.

"Death Star plans," said Vijay.

"Okay. And?"

"And they're encrypted," Vijay said. "I need you to pull out that laptop you don't have and find out what we've got here."

"Okay, hang on," he said. He put on a pair of gloves, grabbed a kitchen knife from a drawer, and went into the washroom. He used the knife to pull out the edge of the tub surround. Behind it was a board which also came out, revealing the elevator shaft. He crawled in, made his way across old pipes to the other side, lay down, and reached behind and under a ventilation shaft. When he pulled his hand out again, he was holding a leather laptop envelope.

Back in the living room, he fired up the laptop and inserted the flash drive.

"Can you break the encryption?" Vijay asked.

"Jeez, I don't know, this is pretty high level."

"How long do you think it'll—"

"Done."

"Seriously?" said Katya.

"Yeah, this was not encrypted by a professional, that's for sure," said Amar.

"So what is it?" Rose asked.

"Looks like spreadsheets, mostly. There are also some text documents and pictures," Amar said, opening a spreadsheet to reveal a list of names followed by strings of numbers. "What's all this?"

"I know that name," said Katya, pointing at one on the list. "Scott Fitches. He's a judge or something, isn't he?"

"Yeah, I think he is," said Vijay. "And look, there's Denise Kaylock. That's the coroner, right?"

"Yeah, it is," said Katya.

"But what are those numbers?" Rose said.

"Bank accounts," said Katya.

"Are you sure?" Amar asked.

"Positive. That's one of ours."

"That doesn't look like any transit number I've ever seen," said Amar, pointing to a different number on the list.

"That's because it's in the Caymans," Katya said.

Amar ran a search for Scott Fitches and found a folder full of pictures. "I'll bet I can guess what these are of," he said, opening one. "Yup."

"Hey, I think that's my barista," Vijay said.

Amar moved to another picture and everyone's head tilted to the left in an attempt to parse what they were seeing.

"Oh, my," said Katya.

"Yep, that's him," said Vijay.

"Limber," said Rose.

"I have to know what's up with Kaylock," said Katya.

Amar ran ran a search and found a folder full of surveillance photos of her trading a cooler for a briefcase.

"She's selling organs?" Rose asked.

"It certainly looks that way," Vijay said.

"You guys didn't..." Rose began.

"No," Katya said, and then the full realization of what Rose was asking hit her, and she repeated the "No!" much more emphatically. "No, of course not." Then to Vijay, she said, "We didn't, did we?"

"We did not," he said. "I mean, I would have if I needed to. For you. But I didn't."

"Okay," said Rose. "Just checking."

They continued poking around through folders, looking up names on the Internet, and finding all sorts of people, most of them wealthy and/or powerful.

"Jesus, Sam's got dirt on every lawyer, judge, business owner... Anyone with a modicum of power in the county," said Katya.

"And they're all paying into this same account," said Vijay.

"Which we now have access to," said Amar.

"Do we want that?" Katya asked.

"The kind of money that's in this account?" Amar said. "Yes. Yes, we want that. Very much."

"But we could use this to bring Sam down for good," Katya said.

"And send me to jail until I'm old and useless like Vijay," said Amar. "Not to mention you being on the run from his allies for the rest of your natural lives."

"Does he even have allies?" said Rose.

"A guy like that always has allies," Amar said. "As long as they're useful to him."

"I don't know," said Katya. "Vijay?"

"We don't technically need the money," he said. "But..."

"Rose?" said Katya.

"I literally just want them dead."

"Well, that got dark fast," said Amar. "I approve."

"I don't know," said Katya. "Why don't we go back to my parents' place and consider our next move?"

Rose and Vijay agreed.

"Can you pass me the drive?" Katya asked.

Amar pulled the flash drive and handed it to her.

"Thanks, Amar," she said. "This is huge."

"Don't mention it," he said. "Let me know what you decide. Or maybe don't. Depending. I don't know."

"Okay, well, we should probably get our new friend here back to the airport," said Vijay.

"I kind of don't want to miss this," said Cecilia.

"You're not safe, though," said Rose. "I really appreciate you helping but you've already done more than enough."

Forty-Two

Cecilia was dropped off at the airport with many hugs and promises to keep in touch.

That evening at Katya's parents' place, the flash drive sat on the coffee table. Katya, Rose, and Vijay sat around it.

"It's a lot of responsibility," said Vijay.

"If this gets out, it could ruin a lot of people," Katya said.

"Maybe they deserve to be ruined," said Vijay.

"What about the innocent bystanders?" said Katya. "The spouses and the children?"

"I hadn't thought of them," said Vijay.

"I mean, even if we use this to bring down Sam, it'll still come back on those people," she said.

"That's if it even gets to that," said Vijay. "If this gets into the hands of a judge or someone who's on that list, they'll likely just destroy it. And maybe even kill us since we know."

"I don't want to end up dead," said Katya. "No offense."

"None taken," said Rose.

Katya's phone vibrated. "It's Cecilia," she said and answered it. "Hey. Did you get home safe?"

"No, she did not," said a voice.

"Sam?" Katya stood up. Vijay and Rose gasped.

"Say hello," said Sam.

"Katya, I'm sorry," came the voice of Cecilia. "They found me at the—"

"I want the flash drive," said Sam.

"What if I don't have it?"

"For your sake, you'd better," said Sam. "If not, you and your friend here and everybody you care about are dead. I've got units stationed at all exits from the city, so you can't run. And if you try, it won't go well for you. Do you understand me?"

"Yeah," she said. "I understand."

"Good. I want you to go to the corner of Rural Route 6 and Wilson Avenue. Be there in forty minutes. Bring the flash drive and come alone. I have eyes everywhere. If I get word that there's anybody else with you, your friend dies. If that ghost bitch appears anywhere, your friend dies. If I see anything I don't like, your friend dies. Got it?"

"Yeah, I got it."

He hung up.

"What do we do?" said Rose.

"I guess I have to go."

"You can't go alone," said Vijay.

"I don't see what other choice I have."

Forty-Three

Thirty-eight minutes later, Katya arrived at the intersection of Rural Route 6 and Wilson Avenue. Her headlights illuminated a strip of reflective tape stuck to a tree on the corner. It held a piece of paper.

She got out of her car, looked around cautiously, and pulled the note off of the tree. In shaky handwriting, it read, *Old schoolhouse. 1/4 mile east. Come on foot. Alone. You are being watched.* Alone was underlined twice.

She did as the note said, constantly looking over her shoulder and peering into the woods, wondering whether she was actually being watched or not.

The old schoolhouse was a brown brick relic from the 1960s. The parking lot was cracked and overgrown with weeds. Most of the windows were smashed out. The front door was propped open with a chair.

She walked up to the front door and peered inside. Foliage snaked its way through the broken windows and had begun to take hold in cracks in the floor. The remains of an old campfire sat cold in the middle of the hallway, the ceiling above it blackened. Graffiti covered every surface.

She stepped inside and looked around. There was no sign of Sam or Bradley or anybody else. Was the whole thing fake? Had they sent her on a wild goose chase in order to get her out of the way? But for what reason? Rose was the one with the powers, not her.

"Nice of you to come," said a voice, echoing throughout the building.

Kai stood to her right, at the top of the stairway to the second-floor addition. He held a gun in one hand, a crutch in the other.

"This way," he said.

She walked up the stairs and he stepped aside to let her pass him. Down the hallway and to the left, a faint light spilled from a classroom. She entered to find Bradley standing beside Sam, who was holding Cecilia with one hand. In his other hand, he held a gun pressed against the back of her head. Her arms were cuffed behind her back and she was blindfolded. The room was lit by a battery-powered lantern, leaving most of the place in shadows.

"Kat?" she said.

"Are you okay?" Katya said. "Have they hurt you?"

"I'm sorry, Katya," said Cecilia. "They grabbed me at the airport."

"I thought it was odd she wasn't dead any more," said Kai, behind Katya.

"Good thing he was picking up a client at the time," said Bradley. "Otherwise you might have gotten away with it."

"Here's the drive," Katya said, holding it out. "Give me Cecilia."

"Give it to Bradley," said Sam.

"Let her go, first."

"No. You give the drive to Bradley."

"How do I know you'll let her go?"

"You don't," said Sam. "But you've got no choice. You give it to him or I kill both of you. And your brother-in-law."

"That wasn't part of the deal," said a voice from the shadows behind her. She turned to see Amar in the corner behind the open door, holding a metal briefcase. He stepped into the light.

"It'd solve your problems with your bookie pretty quick, though," said Sam. "Then they'll likely just go after your brother."

"Amar?" said Katya.

"Sorry, Kat," he said. "Just give him the key and all this will be over soon."

She stared at him, open-mouthed, unable to speak. Finally, she handed the drive to Bradley.

"Fine," she said. "Can we go now?"

"Hardly," said Sam. "Kai?"

Kai reached under a desk, retrieved a briefcase, and slid it across the floor to Amar. He opened it to reveal a very large sum of cash. Amar slid his own briefcase across the floor to Kai.

Kai opened it and retrieved something wrapped in cloth. He unwrapped it to reveal an ornate silver dagger with an eight-inch, wavy, black blade.

"Give it to Bradley," Sam said. Kai handed it to him. Sam pushed Cecilia across the room to Kai and pointed the gun at Katya. He grabbed her, spun her around, took a handful of her hair, and jammed the gun into the side of her head. He stuck his leg between hers and pushed his foot down hard on top of hers so she couldn't move. "Trade," he said to Bradley, and handed him the gun in exchange for the knife.

He held it in front of her face and said, "You know what this is?"

"A knife?" she said.

"With a blade made of meteor. The only way to stop Rose," said Amar. "A meteor dagger in her heart."

"Killing me in the process."

"I'm sorry, Kat," Amar said. "But you're already on borrowed time."

"I can't believe you'd do this to me," said Katya.

"You think I'm doing this for me?" he said. "This is payback for what you did to Uncle Raj."

"Uncle Raj. Of course," she said.

"If you two are done," Sam said, and he held the blade to her chest.

"I can't watch this," Amar said, and he grabbed his cash and walked towards the door.

"Coward!" Katya yelled, as Sam brought the blade down to her chest.

And it shattered.

Amar spun around and threw the briefcase. It connected with Bradley's head and he fell backwards. The gun went off, sending the bullet into the ceiling. As the briefcase hit its target, Amar pulled the blindfold off of Cecilia's head. It took a moment for her eyes to adjust, during which time Sam pushed Katya away from him. He grabbed the gun from Bradley, pointed it at Katya, and pulled the trigger.

Rose appeared between them and the bullet hit her square in the chest.

She looked down at the hole where her heart used to be, then looked at Sam and shrugged.

Kai fired his gun as well, and put another bullet into Rose.

Amar dove for Kai but Katya had already jumped in front of him, her back to him, and put one hand on his forearm and the other on his gun hand. She twisted the gun upwards as hard as she could, breaking his trigger finger. He screamed and stepped backwards. Katya, her hand still wrapped around the gun, brought her hand down, disarming him.

She stepped to the side and pointed the gun at Sam.

"You're going to kill me?" said Sam. "I hardly think so."

"No, but Rose is," Katya said.

"I don't think she is. After all, she can't," he said, turning to Rose. "Can you?"

"I killed Blaine," she said.

"Yeah, you did," he said. "But not me. Or Bradley. Despite the fact that you've had all kinds of chances. You aren't here to kill me. You're just here to scare me. Well, I ain't scared. But you should be."

He pointed the gun at Katya.

"Do it, Dad," said Bradley.

"He won't," said Rose. "He can't explain this many bodies."

"Sure he can," said Bradley. "We own this town. He'll have her death ruled an accident. Same way he had yours ruled an accident after I pushed you down the stairs. Same way he faked the ballistics report on her and her baby."

"You what?" said Katya.

"Yeah, so what?" said Sam. "It was your own fault for getting between me and a bank robber. And as for you," he said, turning to Rose.

Katya pulled the trigger. And missed.

Sam flinched and brought his gun around to face Katya. Rose grabbed his arm and pulled it towards her. He screamed and pulled the trigger. The bullet hit Kai in the good leg. He screamed and collapsed. Blood sprayed from an artery.

Sam's arm smoked, shriveled, and turned black.

"Thank you for finally admitting it," she said, as the

blackness spread to his neck and face. His scream cut out as his head turned to ash. She dropped him and turned to Bradley.

"Your turn," she said.

He spun around and jumped out the window. Rose watched him land in a tree and go careening to the ground. When he landed, he turned to find her in his face.

"Boo!" she said.

He screamed and ran, forcing his way through the overgrown plants. She followed slowly behind.

Upstairs, Katya wiped her fingerprints off the gun.

"You okay?" she asked Amar.

"Yeah, you?" Amar said.

"I think so. Cecilia?"

Cecilia nodded. "Yeah. I mean no, but I'm alive."

"I'm really sorry about all of this," Katya said. "I never wanted to put you in any real danger."

"I know," said Cecilia. "But I knew it was dangerous when I said yes. I mean, I feel like I kind of owed her."

"I know what you mean."

"Question," said Cecilia. "Why aren't you beating Amar to death? Did you plan all this out?"

"Nope," said Katya. "It was all about Uncle Raj."

"Who the hell is Uncle Raj?"

Katya and Amar laughed.

"He's a guy in a frame," Katya said.

"I'm sorry?"

"My mom bought a bunch of frames at the dollar store to hang up pictures of the family in the living room," Amar said. "But she bought more than she needed so she hung one up with the display picture still in it."

"As a joke, she decided he was Uncle Raj," said Katya. "And everybody just went with it."

"Family in-jokes as code," said Cecilia. "That's kind of awesome."

"Speaking of the family joke, we should call Vijay. Let him know we're alive," said Amar.

Forty-Four

Bradley ran down the road, his lungs heaving and his legs burning. Every time he looked behind him, she was there, walking calmly.

"I'm sorry," he called out. "I'll do anything! Anything you ask!"

But she ignored his pleas and just kept walking.

He approached a corner, turned to look behind him, and saw her calmly walking towards him. He turned the corner, looked behind him, and there she was, only feet away. He kept running.

He ran and ran but it was no use. Finally, he collapsed. His legs wouldn't move anymore. He crawled, dragging himself along the road, until his hands and knees were bloody.

Rose appeared beside him.

"Don't," he said, crying. "Please don't. I'm sorry. I'm so sorry. I shouldn't have pushed you. But I couldn't stand seeing you talking to that guy."

"What guy?"

"At the coffee shop," he said. "You were talking to a

guy. You were sitting together."

Rose thought about it for a moment.

"The guy with the long hair?" she said. "In the leather jacket?"

"Yes," he said. "I don't care anymore. It's fine. Just don't kill me."

"That was Jarred," she said. "My brother."

He stared at her and blinked.

"Your brother?" he said.

"Stand up."

"I can't."

"Stand... Up!"

He dragged himself to his feet and stood, wobbling.

"Step off the side of the cliff," she said.

He looked behind him at the cliff, the river flowing along at the base of it.

"Step off the cliff," she said. "It's not that far, and there are bushes. If you live, you're free to go. If not? Well, either way, you're rid of me."

He considered the offer and decided he'd risk it. He stepped off the side of the cliff, aiming for the water. But his legs were too tired and he came up short and landed in a bush. He was still alive. He looked up to see Rose watching from above.

"I'm alive!" he said. "I made it! I'm free to go, right? You said! You promised!"

"You can go," she said.

He laughed in relief and started to climb out of the bush, but a thorn caught his shirt. He tugged at it, and the thorn dug in deeper, tearing his flesh. The more he struggled, the more thorns dug into him, scraping his flesh and drawing blood to the surface. Soon he was unable to move. Thorns scraped against his bones and blood oozed down the branches. All the while Rose stood at the top of the cliff, watching.

Headlights fell upon her. She turned away and got into the car.

Forty-Five

They arrived at Katya's mom's house to find Vijay already waiting out front. He gave Katya a huge hug the second she got out of the car, then jumped back.

"Sorry," he said.

"You're apologizing for hugging me?"

"Well, you know," he said, pointing at her chest. "Healing."

"Nah, I'm okay," she said.

"Cecilia? Rose? Are you both okay?"

They assured him that they were fine.

"I'm fine, too, by the way," said Amar.

"What are you doing here?"

"It's a long story." He held up the briefcase and said, "But I'm definitely good."

"Well, let's all go inside," said Vijay. "You can tell me what happened."

They all approached the house except for Rose.

"Rose?" Katya said. "You coming?"

They all stopped and turned to look at her.

"No. I have to go."

"Go?" Katya asked. "Go where?"

"Back," she said.

"You mean...?"

"Yeah."

"Oh," said Katya. "Are you sure?"

"Yeah," Rose said, nodding. "I'm done what I came here to do. Thank you. Thank you all."

They all nodded, but said nothing.

"I'll give you a ride," said Katya.

"No," said Rose. "Thanks, but I'd like to walk."

"It's a long way."

"That's okay," said Rose. "I'm not in a hurry. But I do have to go."

"Okay," said Katya.

Rose turned to leave, but stopped and turned back. "Katya?"

"Yes?"

"I'm glad it was you who got my heart."

"It's a good one," said Katya.

And she watched Rose walk away, into the pre-dawn fog, until she disappeared out of sight.

Forty-Six

Katya and Vijay drove through downtown Port Hackett, listening to the news on the radio.

"It's been one year since the grisly and bizarre deaths of three prominent members of the community, including the apparent burning of Police Sheriff Samuel Wagner after allegedly killing Kai Takahashi, a friend of the sheriff's son Bradley who was, the same night, found dead of abrasions caused by falling into a rose bush on Rural Route 6. All of this just a day after the mysterious disappearance of another friend of Wagner and Takahashi, Blaine Carstairs, a promising young lawyer at Wagner and Browne, a firm co-owned by the mother and widow of two of the deceased.

"Authorities have no leads on the case, although they believe it's related to a flash drive mailed anonymously to the FBI. A flash drive the contents of which have rocked this community..."

Vijay shut off the radio as they pulled into a spot in front of By Any Other Name, which was showing off a fancy new sign and spruced up frontage.

"I'll just be a moment," Katya said.

"It's all good," Vijay said. "We've got lots of time."

Katya went into the florist's and found Iris Kaidan arranging stock behind a new counter.

"Hello," she said. "Oh, Katya, it's you."

"Hi, Iris," she said. "Wow, the place looks great."

"Thank you. It's all thanks to my mysterious benefactor," Iris said.

"You never found out who it was?"

"Nope," Iris said. "'An anonymous angel investor,' is what the lawyer said. "I mean, who just gives a bunch of cash to a struggling florist?"

"That's so weird, but it's pretty amazing!"

"It really is," Iris said. "I wish I knew who it was. I want to thank them. Let them know how much it's appreciated."

"Oh, I'm sure they know," said Katya.

"I don't know if they know how close I was to shutting this place down," Iris said. "I was so depressed after Rose died and I just couldn't deal. I couldn't get out of bed some days."

"Well, maybe this'll be a second chance for you."

"It will," she said, nodding. "I guess somebody up there likes me."

"Of that, I have no doubt," said Katya.

"I mean, I still miss Rose, of course. I always will. But it's time to move on."

"That's what she'd want for you," said Katya.

"I'm sure she would," Iris said. "And how are you? How's the new place? Are you all settled in?"

"It's great," Katya said. "We spent last weekend painting."

"So I saw. The red trim looks amazing," said Iris. "And that door really pops."

"Thanks," said Katya. "We're very happy with it."

Katya bought a small bouquet, went back to the car, and drove to the graveyard. They parked and Vijay opened the back door to remove a tiny human from her baby seat. She squirmed and made fussy noises.

Holding hands, they walked along the rows of headstones until they found the one they were looking for. Katya set the bouquet on top of it.

They sat down and Vijay held the baby up as if the stone could see it.

"Hi, Rose," Katya said. "I'd like you to meet Rose. We named her after a good friend who helped us through a hard time."

They sat in silence for a moment, baby Rose gurgling and kicking her feet.

In front of the headstone, between it and the young family, the ground shook just slightly. A green tendril poked up from the earth and snaked and twisted its way up into the air about six inches. The tendril thickened and the top end widened into a bulb, which spiraled open and turned toward them. Petals spread out, revealing themselves for what they were: a single, perfect rose.

About the Author

Mike Bryant was once ejected from a karaoke bar for performing the Weird Al Yankovic classic "Yoda", instead of Taking Things Seriously.

His novella *Operation Dickhead* was published by Burning Effigy Press and he won the 2014 Shitty Poetry Competition with his poem "A Stark and Wormy Blight".

Mike is the only human member of nerd rock band Kraken Not Stirred.

CPSIA information can be obtained
at www.ICGtesting.com
Printed in the USA
LVHW031842060421
683591LV00003B/638

9 781928 011484